Love from Farm to Stable

Book 2 *Over the Bay Series*

Deborah McDonald

Love from Farm to Stable

ISBN: 978-1-954693-11-1

FV 10

Printed in the United States

This is the second book in the Over the Bay Series.

www.IntellectPublishing.com

Acknowledgments

I'm happy to tell my readers that the second book in the Over the Bay Series is here!

I would like to thank my family for supporting me with their patience as I spent many hours burning the midnight oil at the computer and so glad you all know how to sleep through my clicking of the keys on the laptop at 2 AM. Emma, Amanda, Eva and Olivia, I think you are all wonderful and have an amazing future ahead. You are true ladies, and we are so proud of all of you. To my husband, who's a great dad to all the girls. Thank you, Owen, for all of your support, sense of humor and love throughout the years (Getting engaged at Beaver Pond was one of the highlights of our years together.)

Thank you to my siblings Linda, Paul and Laurie and all of the fun trips to NOLA. Here's to many more in the future. I appreciate the medical advice you have given me to help my characters heal. To the family in what I like to call the other part of the SEC! Thanks for the football texting Saturdays, the jokes and birthday fun!

Thank you to my collaborator/editor, Deborah Navarro. She has brought so much to the books in this series with ideas for dialogue and frequent checks on grammar/punctuation. I love her idioms! She has been a good friend over the years. She's just amazing.

Thank you to Julia Taylor, for the fabulous book cover. You are a true artist!

Andy Jones, I can't thank you enough for all the advice about farming. Your extensive knowledge of farming is truly AU-SOME (yes, that spelling is just for you!)—Any mistakes in the interpretation of your conversation with me are all mine!

Thank you to Aunt Wilma for answering questions about life on a farm growing up. The stories about your ancestors inspired me to write this book.

Speech Language Pathologists---I appreciate your time on the weekends answering my questions to help me navigate the process of how to become an SLP. Y'all do a tremendous job working with students.

To all the educators and school staff who work at all hours of the day and night to ensure student success! Thank you to my oldest friends, who have stuck with me, eaten with me, celebrated with me, gone to events with me, and listened to me talk A LOT over the years! You know who you are!

Thank you to the members of the Pensters! What a great group of writers!

And as always, thank you John O'Melveny Woods, publisher extraordinaire.

Deborah McDonald

Love from Farm to Stable

Book 2 *Over the Bay Series*

Love from Farm to Stable

Chapter 1

The atmosphere was festive inside the Hospitality Center at Jubilee Sunset Theme Park. The owner of the park and his new bride had just left the building in a cascade of bubbles. Karen Smith, the bride's sister, had caught the bouquet. She breathed in the heady scent of the flowers. Not that catching the flowers at a wedding meant anything to her. She had spent so much time studying to earn her master's degree that she really hadn't dated much at all. She always wondered if the few guys she dated were more interested in her looks than her intelligence. Her sister, Florence, always told her she resembled Audrey Hepburn, with her long brown hair swept up in a bun, thin frame, and classic looks.

"Well, look at you," said a voice from behind her. Hunt, short for Dr. George Huntington, winked at her as she turned to face him, "You caught the bouquet. Good for you."

She smiled, "I'm afraid these flowers are meant for a vase, nothing else."

He grinned back at her, "Well, you're still young so you have time. You're not old like me."

"Seriously?" she smiled.

"Yes, seriously. People call me at 9PM and say, "Did I wake you?" He smiled at her.

She shook her finger at Hunt, "Yes, my sister Florence warned me about your sense of humor."

"Oh, you mean, how funny I am?"

She shook her head with a twinkle in her eye, "No, that's not how I took it."

Hunt chuckled. She bent her head to smell the bouquet. Hunt looked around the room, "You know, I've seen several pairs of eyes look your way from more than one gentleman here tonight." Hunt rocked back on his heels, "If I may say so, you look very pretty."

Karen glanced down at the blue chiffon dress that matched Hunt's blue tie, "Thank you," she said. The Hospitality Center was arranged for the wedding with white linen cloths covering tables and elegant fall arrangements of flowers on each table. She noticed the gift tables bulging with packages of all sizes and shapes. She was tasked with taking the gifts to her sister's apartment. She didn't realize how many presents there would be and wasn't sure how she was going to get them all in her car.

Hunt followed her gaze and stared at the presents, "I'll be more than happy to help you."

At that moment, a man approached her, "Karen, hello. I've been meaning to come and talk to you, but you've been busy." She focused on the face of Curtis Dalton, the brother of her sister's late fiancé, Keith, who died three years ago. He was about ten years older than her. He reminded her of a young Kevin Costner with his rugged good looks. He was a farmer with one of the biggest farms in Baldwin County.

She had seen him some when she would go with Florence to visit the farm. Of course, since his brother's death, she hadn't seen him in a few years, "Curtis, hello. I don't think you've met Hunt, who was Riley's best man."

He shook Hunt's hand, "No, I don't believe I have. Nice to meet you."

"Same here," said Hunt.

She explained, "Curtis is an old family friend."

He glanced at her, "Thanks a lot for putting the word "old" in that introduction." He winked and smiled at her. She smiled and blushed.

"Well," Hunt glanced from Karen to Curtis, "It looks like the party is breaking up. Do you want me to help you load the presents? I just have to run to the bungalow to get my car." She gazed at the stack of endless bags and boxes of wrapped gifts.

Before she could answer Curtis said, "Hey, I have my SUV outside if that would help. I bet all of these would fit. Where are you heading with them?"

She gazed at all the presents, "To Florence's apartment."

At that moment, they heard a ringtone on Hunt's phone, "I'm sorry. That's the hospital. I'm taking a shift for a colleague tonight." He studied Curtis, "If you can help, that would be great." He nodded. Hunt gave her a hug, "It was a fun day." With a quick thank you, he was gone.

She looked at Curtis and explained, "Hunt's a doctor and has been best friends with Riley for years. They live next to each other at the Bungalows in the back of the park."

He nodded, "Ready?"

She walked over with him to the tables. Several employees met them there and offered to help carry the presents to his car. She saw her mom, Janet and her fiancé, Ed Howard, gathering the flowers from the table. Riley's mom and his Aunt Alice were taking care of boxing up the cake. She called out to them and said she was going with Curtis to take the gifts to Florence's apartment. Her mom and Ed hugged her and told her how pretty she looked today, and they would see her at home. Karen waved to Aunt Alice and Riley's mom.

She walked out of the building and realized she should have brought a wrap to put around her shoulders. It was going to be one of those November nights in Alabama in which it was 75 degrees some nights and in the 50's other nights. This was one of those other nights. As she reached his vehicle, he was waiting to open the door for her. That was a nice change. Usually, the few men that she had dated had never opened her door for her, "Thank you." As she passed him, she couldn't help but notice his cologne. He smelled good. Now where did that thought come from? Maybe she could attribute her thoughts to her lack of going out on any dates the last few months.

He got into the car and started the engine. He looked over and noticed that she was shivering. He reached in the back seat and picked up his jacket he kept in the car for when he had to check on things around the farm at night. It could get chilly. He handed it to her. When she had trouble getting it around her shoulders, he offered, "Here, let me help."

She leaned forward as he slipped the jacket around her shoulders. The jacket caught her pins in her hair, causing it to tumble around her shoulders. His gaze followed the motion of her hair falling. His hand was still on her shoulder. She shook her hair out of her eyes. She was face to face with him. He cleared his throat and moved back to his seat. She took a deep breath. Curtis backed out of the parking lot and headed to Florence's apartment. As he drove, they talked about the wedding.

She glanced at him, "I thought that was nice of your family to come to the wedding today. That couldn't have been easy for you."

He sighed, "We wanted to be here for Florence. She spent so much time with Keith at the farm and we've missed having her there. I'm glad she found someone. My brother would have wanted her to have a life with someone to love."

She took a deep breath and responded, "When Florence would bring me to the farm, I really didn't get to see all of it and what you do there. I remember fields and fields of green. I always thought with the size of your farm, you would never run out of fields. I just know Florence told me it has been in your family for years. Your land always reminded me of Ireland."

He glanced at her and smiled, "Have you ever been to Ireland?"

"No," her eyes showed amusement, "I only know about the fields in Ireland because of pictures in travel magazines or what I've seen in movies. I wouldn't mind going someday, though."

She peered back at him, "How about you? Ever travel out of the country?"

"Mom and Dad always talked about taking us kids overseas to England, Scotland and Ireland. It was one of those package deals, but life was so busy with them running the farm and us helping them. There just never seemed to be a good time."

She smiled back at him, "Have you always wanted to be a farmer?"

"Actually, I got a business degree when I went to college and was on my way to being hired by one of the major corporations in Birmingham."

"What happened?" she asked.

He was quiet for a minute and cleared his throat, "Mom was diagnosed with cancer. Keith was still in college, so I came home to run the farm."

"From what I remember, I think Florence did mention that your mom was in remission?" asked Karen.

He smiled, "Yes, she is, and I'm thankful every day."

"Did you ever think of leaving the farm when she got better?" she asked. He stopped for a red light.

"Well, by that time, I was settled, and Keith was on his way to finishing his degree in Agribusiness. So, I thought it would be nice to run the farm with him."

A melancholy look passed over his face. Without thinking, she put her hand on top of his that was resting on his lap. Gazing at her, he realized she was a beautiful woman with intelligent green eyes that at this moment showed concern for him. He remembered that this was Florence's sister, who was considerably younger than him and from what he remembered a very sweet person. She was just being nice. He squeezed her hand and let it go, "Thank you," he said.

She put her hand back on her lap and was quiet for the rest of the drive. All too soon, he pulled up to Florence's apartment and the gifts were emptied out of his car. As he stood at the door, he asked her if he could drop her back home. She replied that she was going to call her mom to let her know that she would just spend the night at Flo's and ask her mom to take her to work in the morning. Karen told him sometimes she spent the night at her sister's apartment and always kept a change of clothes there.

He asked, "Where do you work?" She told him about the coffee shop where she worked until she graduated from college. He thought for a minute and offered, "Listen, I'm going in that direction in the morning. Why don't I pick you up and drop you off at work? It would save your mom a trip."

She didn't know how to answer him. He was so nice and such a gentleman. She thought about it, "Okay, if you're sure you don't mind."

"Mind?" he replied, "I have an ulterior motive. I was hoping you sold doughnuts at that coffee shop of yours." She smiled so brightly that her whole face lit up. He thought again how beautiful she was, and how he was going to be in trouble if he didn't stop thinking this way about Florence's little sister.

"We do. Since you've been such a big help tonight, how about a coffee and a doughnut in the morning as my treat?"

He gazed at those beautiful green eyes, "That's an offer I can't refuse." He walked out of the apartment door and turned back to look at her. She told him what time she needed to be at work. "I'll see you in the morning. I'm going to stand out here until I hear you lock up." He raised his hand to wave, "Goodnight." He heard the lock engage and returned to his SUV. He'd never looked forward to a morning quite like this before. He told himself he was only being nice because she was Florence's sister. He thought if he said it often enough, maybe he would believe it.

Chapter 2

I t was still dark when Curtis pulled up to Florence's apartment the next morning. He pulled his ball cap on and headed for the door. He knocked while blowing on his hands clasped together as it was a chilly morning. Turning to look at his surroundings, he heard the door open. As he turned back, he remembered how beautiful she was last night all dressed up for her sister's wedding. This morning, she was stunning with her face cleanly scrubbed, her eyes bright and her hair pulled back in a ponytail. She was dressed in a black t-shirt, black leggings, and black tennis shoes.

"Hi," she said as she smiled at Curtis.

"Hi, yourself. Are you ready to go?"

"Yes," she answered, as she grabbed a black and red apron with a store logo printed on the front, "Oh, hang on." She went back into the apartment. She was pulling on a white and blue ball cap with a school logo on the front, "Okay, I'm ready." She locked the door, turned, and ran smack into him. He put his hands up on her arms to steady her, "Sorry," she said, "I didn't realize you hadn't moved."

He released his arms from hers, "Not a problem. I'm just not sure I can let you in my truck."

She asked, "Oh, what's the matter with the truck?"

There was a serious expression lingering on his face, "Nothing's wrong with my truck. It's that hat you're wearing."

She touched her hat with the logo of a jaguar, "Oh, it's going to be like that, is it?"

"Yes ma'am," He touched his ball cap which displayed the big letters of his alma mater, 'AU'. "This is the only school that really matters. Did you happen to see the size of our stadium?"

"You do know my university just built a new stadium."

"Sure, if that's what you want to call it."

She replied, "Tell you what. Why don't we agree to disagree? At least neither one of us is wearing a crimson hat with that big ridiculous elephant on the front. Karen continued as she pointed to their caps, "Tigers and Jaguars, aren't those cooler and stealthier than a big old, wrinkled tusker?"

He studied her and moved to open her door for her, "Okay, you make a lot of sense." Once she was seated, he shut the truck door. He shook his head and grinned as he walked around the truck and climbed in his seat and said, "Tusker? That's a new one," he laughed.

He pulled up to the coffee shop with the sign that said, *Good to the Last Drop*. He checked out the big coffee cup tilting sideways with a drop of coffee dripping out of

16

the cup, "Hang on," He got out of his truck to walk around to her side to open the door for her.

She focused on him and said, "Thank you. I'm just not used to men being this chivalrous."

He responded, "Anytime."

She got out her key to open the front door. After they were both inside, she turned and locked the door. He saw all the various bags of coffee and teas displayed in the store. She put on her apron and began to prep for the morning, "What kind of coffee would you like?" she asked him.

"Oh, I'm a regular cup of coffee kind of guy with nothing added but straight up coffee," He smiled at her.

"Okay, how about an adventure today? Do you see how many kinds of coffee we have? Don't you want to try something different than what you have every day?"

He glimpsed at her earnest face, excited for him to try something new, "You don't know how this is a life changing event for me. I never allow anyone to touch my coffee." She was watching him expectantly, "Okay. I leave my coffee in your hands." He sat at a table and watched her as she scooped, measured, ground the coffee, and added something to the grounds before brewing the coffee. Then he watched her plate a donut and walk the donut and coffee to the table. She stood there and folded her arms over her chest.

His eyes met hers, "You're actually waiting for me to drink this in front of you?" she nodded, and he asked, "What if I don't like it?"

"Then I will think less of you and make you a boring cup of black coffee," she replied. He blew on the coffee and sipped from the cup. He tasted a flavor he couldn't quite put his finger on. He glanced at her as she was still watching him. She really did have the prettiest green eyes. He took a big breath, held the coffee cup and then gazed at her.

"You don't like it, do you?" His eyes travelled to his coffee cup. "It's okay," she said, "you can be honest. I'm a big girl. I can take it." He cleared his throat. She seemed so excited for him to try something new that he hated to hurt her feelings.

He finally answered as his eyes rose to hers, "I appreciate you trying to bring me into this century regarding coffee, but I'm a creature of habit." His eyes crinkled and he smiled. She didn't realize, until this moment in being this close to him, that his eyes were the warmest shade of brown.

Curtis asked, "So, what's in it?"

She smiled, "Nutmeg and cinnamon that I sprinkled on the coffee grounds."

He smiled inwardly at her excitement. It took such a little thing to make her happy. He would like to see her happy more often. He knew what her and Florence's lives were like when they were younger, being abused by their uncle. He understood that uncle was now dead. Good riddance to someone who could abuse little girls. She began to clear his coffee cup and his hand reached for the cup at the same time as hers. He said, "I hate to waste it.

18

It's not that bad." He felt her hand tremble slightly as his hand brushed hers. Curtis moved his hand as he glanced into those green eyes, which reminded him of the beautiful green fields at his family farm, "Thank you, Karen."

She lost herself in his warm brown eyes, then cleared her throat, "You're welcome. Do you want that to go? I don't want to keep you if you're supposed to be somewhere."

He checked his watch and told her that would be a good idea. As he watched her skirt the counter to bag his donut and put his coffee in a to-go cup, he realized how much he had enjoyed just being with her and would like to spend time with her again. He really didn't know what a good idea that would be and what would Florence think? They loved each other like brother and sister. He wouldn't want to do anything to change that relationship. He stood as she handed him a bag and a container holding two cups of coffee to go. He raised his eyebrow as she said, "I thought I'd give you a cup of your usual, although you're sweet to want to try to save my feelings over something you didn't like." When the container shifted, she put her hand out, accidentally touching his. His eyes met hers. She couldn't look away and found herself taking a deep breath. She finally was able to say, "Thank you for helping me last night and for bringing me to work."

He asked her how long she was working today, and she told him she was closing the shop that night. Curtis looked at Karen and realized his gaze had traveled from her eyes to her mouth. He cleared his throat. When he reached the door, he turned back one more time with a gleam in his eyes, "Thank you for trying to help me change my ways, but I know what I like." When her eyes widened, he grinned at her, winked, and walked out of the shop.

She felt her knees sinking with the looks he had been giving her. She lowered herself to one of the chairs at the table. She thought about how handsome he was, how he made her feel safe, and how comfortable she felt being around him. Then she thought about Florence. She didn't know what her sister would say if she knew what thoughts she was having about Curtis. Well, she thought, as she got up to turn around the sign to open the shop, she'd just cross that bridge when she came to it. With the way her mind was working, it just might be sooner rather than later.

Chapter 3

T he next Saturday of the following week was terribly busy for Karen with work and school.

She handed over two mocha Frappuccino's to a customer when she began to help the next one in line, "Flo!" Since there were no other customers in line, she came around the counter to hug her sister, "Oh, I'm so glad to see you! How was the honeymoon?"

Florence Simmons wrapped her arms around her sister, "I'm glad to see you too! I think I'm still on the honeymoon! We had such a good time!"

She saw how happy and glowing her sister was and had to remind her, "Uh, Flo, you spent your honeymoon at the park!"

"I know! Isn't that great? We had such a great time staying in one of the Treehouses! When we got there Riley carried me up the steps to the door. Our moms had stocked the Treehouse with enough food to feed an army and Aunt Alice sent over a basket of her wonderful apple muffins. It was heaven! With the running of the park, we didn't really have the time now to go anywhere too far away, but we agreed right after Christmas we'd go somewhere. I'm just not sure where. We are just so happy at the park! Is that crazy sis?"

Karen said, "No, Flo. I'm glad you found someone to truly love you and so glad to see you happy after everything you've been through. Did y'all decide to stay in Riley's bungalow?"

"Yes," Florence said, "for now we are. I wanted to thank you and Curtis for bringing over the presents to the apartment last weekend."

"You're welcome. In fact, Curtis came through here this morning on his way to Mobile. He took a black coffee with him. Doesn't he know there are other ways to make coffee?" Karen grinned.

Florence glanced at her sister, laughed and hugged her again, "No, he's very settled with his routines. I want you to be happy too. Do you have time to sit down and have a coffee with me?"

She saw two customers about to enter the shop, "Tell you what, how about I get you your favorite to go, and we catch up later tonight? I'm closing at 6:00. Maybe you can come to the house and see Mom and Ed as well. I'll be home as soon as I can after closing."

"Okay, "said Florence, "I'll see you tonight," as she took a coffee to go from her sister.

The day flew by. Karen had been at work since 7:00 AM and had 15 minutes left before closing. The other barista had cleaned the coffee stations and the dishes had been washed in the back of the shop. The barista had left for the day. Her boss had come in to check the receipts and she had said goodnight to her and had gone home earlier. So, it was just her left to clean the tables and close the shop. She began wiping down tables when she heard the door open. She focused on a blonde-haired man who looked to be in his early 40's, wearing a business suit, as he walked through the door.

She said, "I'll be with you in a moment, sir," as she wiped down her last table.

She heard a "click" and she looked up to see that the man had locked the door, "Don't you worry. I was waiting until you were alone because I've been watching you all day. We've got all night."

Curtis pulled into the parking lot of *Good to the Last Drop* just to check on Karen. When he stopped to get coffee this morning, she had mentioned closing tonight. His sister, Leslie, used to work in a pizza place late at night in college. He was always worried about her closing at night because the pizza place was right across from the college and she worked late hours. There were times when he would check on her, and she would remind him she was a big girl and could take care of herself. He smiled at the memory. Thankfully, she never had a problem.

He was getting out of his truck when he heard a scream coming from inside the coffee shop, "Karen!" He pulled out his rifle from the safety seat and ran to the door. A man had her cornered against the wall. He didn't think twice. He rammed the butt of his rifle against the glass door, and it shattered. The man turned around just in time to see a rifle pointing at his face. He didn't take his eyes off of the man as Curtis said to Karen, "Hon, I need you to step behind me."

"I'm afraid to move!" She began to sob.

"I'm going to help you, but I need you to be brave for a little while longer and come stand behind me. Come on, you can do it." He never took his eyes off the man as she began to give the man a wide berth until she got behind Curtis. "Hon, I want you to get my phone out of my back pocket and call the police."

She reached into his pocket, her hands shaking and got his phone. He could hear her crying and telling the police what happened. The man began to move, and the rifle stayed steady as Curtis pointed it at the man's face. The man began to talk, "She came onto me. If I even touch foot in jail, I'll be out in no time once I call my lawyer. You're nothing. Do you know how wealthy I am? I can come back into this coffee shop anytime. It's my word against hers."

"Oh," Curtis said, "you have no idea who I am do you?" as he continued to hold the rifle.

"Poor white trash from what it looks like," he scoffed as the man noticed the dirt on Curtis's clothes and the mud on his boots. Sirens could be heard getting closer to the coffee shop.

She was still crying behind him. He had to keep calm and focus on the man. He'd been ready to pull the trigger 10 minutes ago, but he was going to do this by the book.

Detective Drew Myers entered the coffee shop with his gun drawn, "Mr. Dalton, lower your weapon." He motioned for the other policemen to lower their weapons, "Stand down, Mr. Dalton."

The man in the shop said, "Dalton? Dalton farms?" The man leered at Karen, "Well, I see honey. So, you were playing hard to get with me to give it all to the rich farm boy here, huh?" He looked at Curtis who had lowered the rifle to the ground. The man said, "I see now, want to keep it all for yourself? She must be really good in bed."

Curtis turned slightly to look at the detective. He turned back around, punched the man in the face so hard that he could hear bone crunching.

The man doubled over screaming, "You broke my nose, you SOB! You're mine and I'm coming back for her too!" He continued to curse and yell as the policemen cuffed him and took him away.

By this time Detective Myers scrutinized the bruise on Karen's face. She slid down to the floor. Curtis knelt in front of her. He saw the bruise on her cheek and felt a slow simmer of anger. He tamped his feelings down, "Hey, Honey, hey. It's me, Curtis. I'm here."

She began to sob, "Please help me!"

"I'm right here." He looked her in the eyes and asked, "Can I hold you?" She nodded her head and she continued to sob. He sat with his back against the wall and gently cradled her in his arms.

Detective Myers squatted in front of them, "Miss Smith, I've called your sister and brother-in-law. They should be here soon. Do you feel like talking to me and telling me what happened?"

She just shook her head and held on to Curtis, "Please make it all go away! I don't want to talk to anyone. Please!"

He simply held her and smoothed his hand down her hair, "Why don't we see if we can get you to the hospital? I just want to make sure you aren't hurt."

"Mr. Dalton is right, Miss Smith. We can call an ambulance." After a short time had passed, Florence, Riley and Hunt ran into the shop, glass crunching under their shoes.

Florence kneeled next to her sister, "Hey, I'm here."

"Flo? Please make it go away." She moved from Curtis's arms and held onto her sister and cried.

"Curtis? What are you doing here?" asked Florence.

He explained about stopping by the shop on his way home to check on her. He wanted to make sure she got home safely since she had to close the shop.

She squeezed his hand and said, "Thank you for taking care of my sister." He nodded and stood up.

Hunt came and knelt down next to Karen, "Hey, there. I want to see if you would go to the hospital with me so I can make sure you're okay." He looked up at Riley as he noticed the bruise on her cheek.

She sobbed, "He didn't, he didn't…. Curtis got here before," and then she sobbed again.

Karen looked at Hunt as Riley walked over to put a hand on his wife's shoulder and looked at his sister-in law.

"Hey, we're here for you, okay? How 'bout we go with Hunt to the hospital so he can take care of you just to make sure you're okay?"

Her sobs had turned into tears. She looked around at Riley, Flo and Hunt. Then she saw Curtis, whose warm brown eyes met hers. She looked at Flo and asked, "Can Curtis go with me too?"

Florence looked up at him, whose eyes showed remnants of anger which disappeared with compassion when talking to Karen. He said, "Sure, I can do that."

As Florence helped her sister, Detective Myers told Riley that he would be following them to the hospital to take Karen's statement. Riley nodded at the detective and waited for his wife and his sister-in-law. She was being held by her sister when she reached the broken door, "The shop! I have to call my boss."

The detective said, "Already taken care of. One of the officers called and she should be here shortly. My officers will stay here and help your boss," he said as he took a look at the door frame.

Hunt brought the car around to the front door with Florence helping Karen into the back seat. Riley made sure they were settled and closed the door. He got into the front seat and told Curtis which hospital to meet them as they took off. He was about to get in his truck when Detective Myers stopped him, "A moment of your time, please Mr. Dalton."

"I know where you're going with this, Detective, and you know as well as I do that, I don't need a license for a rifle in the state of Alabama. Now, if you don't mind, I'm in a hurry."

"You might want to get your ducks in a row. We just arrested a man who can press charges for assault against you, not to mention pointing a rifle at him." When Curtis was about to speak Drew Myers held up a hand, "Hey, with the circumstances as they are, personally I don't blame you for what you did. I will follow you to the hospital as I need to take your statement as well as Miss Smith's statement."

Curtis nodded, fired up his truck and began to drive to the hospital. He could feel the anger bubbling up once he had settled enough to think back about this night. He had only felt this much anger one other time in his life and that was when his brother had been killed by a drunk driver. The driver walked away with his life, but unfortunately Keith was killed instantly. The driver should have been put away for life, but according to the law, would be released from jail in a few years. He took a deep breath and concentrated on driving to the hospital. When he got there, he discovered Riley and Edward, Janet's fiancé, sitting in the waiting area and went to join them. Riley raised a hand in greeting. Edward nodded.

Curtis asked, "How is she?"

Riley looked at the door Karen had gone through with her mom and Florence. "She's in bad shape. She's still upset." Riley focused on Curtis, "Can you tell me what happened?"

28

He took a seat, "I was heading back to the farm and not too far from the coffee shop, so I decided to check on her since it was dark out and she had to close the shop. I got out of the truck and heard her screaming. The door was locked, so I smashed the glass. The bastard had her cornered, so my rifle pointing at him helped her get away from him."

Edward noticed as Curtis talked that he had his hands in a fisted grip and there was blood on one of his fists, "What happened to your hand?"

"The detective told me to lower my rifle and right about the time I did that, the asshole made a crude comment about Karen, so I hit him. I forgot about my hand."

Riley put his hand on his shoulder, "Thank you." Riley dropped his hand and said, "It's a nice feeling when abusers who hurt women and children get what's coming to them. I don't know if Florence told you what happened to the man who abused them when they were little." He glanced at Edward, "The bastard shot me, but Edward was able to put a bullet in him. He fell into the Delta and got attacked by an alligator. That took care of that."

Curtis nodded, "Yes, she told me. Looks like you made a nice recovery. I'm glad you and Florence found each other. She didn't have the happiest of childhoods and it was a horrible blow when Keith died."

"I'm sorry about your brother. Florence told me," said Riley.

"I appreciate that. It was awfully hard on all of us. We have reminders of Keith all around us."

"The first time I gave Florence a tour of the park, and we rounded the bend by the Founding Farmer's area, she got terribly upset. Now she's happy we have the area in the park. She thanked me, but I didn't find out until later that she was upset because of memories of your brother."

He watched the people come and go in the waiting area and said, "She was always upset that Keith never got to live out his dream of being a farmer. I think they would have done well together if he had lived." He turned to Riley and said, "But when I watch you and Florence it just seems like you were meant to be together."

Riley looked his way, "I'm incredibly lucky. She came to visit me every day I was in the hospital and she was tough on me to get better. It made my recovery easier having her there." Riley took a deep breath, "I wanted to apologize again for being such an ass when I saw you with Florence at the park. She kind of took me to task for how I treated you and explained your relationship. I finally got smart and told her how I felt about her. It was one of the best days of my life."

Curtis clasped his hands together, "Don't give it another thought. I knew then how you felt about each other." Riley nodded and the men fell silent. They stood as Florence and Karen came out of the door into the waiting area. Karen walked quietly up to Curtis. She stepped forward and gave him a hug. He stood very still then tenderly put his arms around her. He looked over her head at Florence, who had tears in her eyes. Riley held her. Janet walked into Edward's arms.

Karen placed her head on his chest, "Thank you. I don't know what I would have done without you." She started crying and clung to him. He embraced her as her tears fell. As time ticked by, she raised her head. He brushed her hair out of her eyes, "Oh, Curtis, I'm sorry. I didn't mean to cry all over your shirt."

His mouth turned up, "It's okay. It's not my favorite." A smile reached her eyes, but then a shadow fell over her face and she released him. He covered her bruise with his hand. Her sister came to stand beside them, and he included her in the conversation, "We're all here for you. Just remember that. I'm going to have Florence send my number to you in case you want to talk." His eyes met hers, "That means day or night, okay?"

She inclined her head in acknowledgement. Janet walked up to Curtis, "Do you mind if I give you a hug for saving my daughter's life?" He moved forward and gave her a hug. Tears fell from her face, "Thank you so much," She raised her head, "You've always been so kind to my girls." He nodded as he let her go.

Florence put her arm around Karen and said to both men, "Hunt would like to see you in the back please." She pointed to the door she and her sister came through. Riley asked Edward to join them. When they walked through the door, they were met by Hunt and Detective Myers. Hunt took the lead and said, "Detective, before you talk to Curtis, I'm going to clean up his hand if you don't mind."

He hadn't realized anyone noticed his hand. He said, "It's fine. You don't have to bother. I've had worse injuries farming."

"Well," said Hunt, "When someone knocks a good for nothing SOB on his ass and scrapes up his hand doing it, then I tend to want to thank the person by cleaning up his hand. Oh yeah, did I happen to mention no charge?"

Curtis looked from Hunt to Riley and said, "Just to clarify, it was more like a fist in the face which resulted in a broken nose. You see, gentlemen, when you drop someone on their ass, they get a chance to rest. I'd rather get a good hit in and see them double over in pain, especially when they deserve it. It's a lot more satisfying to me that way." Edward agreed with Curtis. Both Riley and Hunt looked at him and smiled. He shifted his stance to look at the detective, "Up to you what you write in your report, but that's how I see things."

The detective stared at Curtis then at Hunt, "Go ahead, doctor, and see to his hand. I can wait." Hunt motioned for Curtis to follow him to a small room.

The two sisters were sitting in the waiting area with their mom. They were sipping hot coffee they got from the coffee machine in the waiting area. Karen was the first to speak, "I make better coffee than this at the shop." Then she realized where her thoughts had taken her. She leaned on Florence's shoulder and let the tears flow. Her sister held her while she cried, "Flo, I can't seem to stop crying." Janet moved to put her arm around her daughter who said, "Oh mom! I was so scared. If Curtis hadn't shown up when he did..." She couldn't finish her thought.

Florence spoke up, "Curtis is a good friend to have. He always seems to know what to say to make things better. Plus, he can have a pretty dry sense of humor at times." She smiled and told Flo what he said about her Jag hat. "Oh, yes," said Florence, "he bleeds orange and blue." They both smiled.

At that point, Riley came out of the door and walked towards them. He sat next to Florence and held her hand. He talked about the detective being there. Janet held Karen tighter and said, "Yes, he talked to her." At that moment, the door opened, and Curtis came out with Detective Myers.

Detective Myers looked at Karen, "Ma'am, I'm sorry you had to go through this tonight." He took a card out of his inside suit pocket, "This is the name of a good therapist on this card in case you need to talk to someone that is not family. Sometimes it's good to talk to a professional." She took the card. He nodded at everyone, "Thank you for your time." He looked at Curtis, "I'll be in touch if I have any further questions. Goodnight."

Curtis watched the detective leave the hospital, then he turned and gazed at Karen. She was looking at him as well. He found out from Riley when they were in the back room that they were taking Karen home, "So," he said, "it looks like it's time to go." He stepped up and put his hand on hers, "Would it be okay if I checked on you tomorrow?"

She placed her other hand on top of his bandaged hand. She glanced at him, "Curtis, what happened to your hand?" Everyone looked at her.

Curtis thought she must have been in shock when in the coffee shop and didn't see him hit the other man, "I just had an injury. Hunt happened to notice it and wrapped it for me. It's all good." With a friendly expression on his face, he managed to say, "I'll be in touch." She nodded her head. He told everyone goodnight and headed for the door.

Chapter 4

The next morning Curtis drove from his house, which happened to be on farm property to what they called the Big House. He pulled up to the house and thought about all the great memories he and his siblings had growing up there. He remembered running through the fields, milking cows, squirting the milk at each other, and riding horses. He smiled. Such great memories. He looked out over the fields which didn't even begin to cover the vastness of their farm. Curtis missed Keith. Sometimes the memories of his brother were so overwhelming he felt he couldn't breathe.

He looked at the stately home. That's how he thought of it. It was a 5,000 square foot brick home with enough rooms to get lost in. He and his siblings would wreak havoc by running through all the rooms, until his mom and dad scooted them outside, usually to work. There was always something to take care of on a farm, that was for sure. Now, it was just his mom and dad here. His sister, Leslie, had her own house on the farm property as well. They were still a close family, despite losing Keith.

He shut off the engine and climbed out of the truck. He looked up and there was his dad waiting on the front porch for him. Curtis climbed the steps and gave his dad a big hug.

Owen Dalton hugged him, "Hey there, Son." His dad looked at Curtis and said, "I went by your house last night because your mom wanted to see if you'd join us for dinner, but you weren't there. We thought you were going to be back last night. Everything go okay in Mobile?" He looked at his dad. For a man in his late 50's, he was still very fit, with a touch of gray threading through his brown hair.

Curtis had inherited the brown eyes from his dad, "Mom inside?" His dad nodded his head, "There's something I'd like to share with you both." They walked through the door and there was his mom. She was taking a breakfast casserole out of the oven. He could always count on his mom for great meals and for both of his parents, really, for always being there. Even through mom's cancer and losing Keith, they always seemed like such a great couple. They had their moments which sometimes meant not speaking to each other over differing opinions, but they were always together. They genuinely loved one another. "Hi, mom," Curtis smiled as he rounded the kitchen table to hug her. Abby Dalton was still beautiful after all these years. Her blonde hair was pulled up in a bun and she wore a crisp white shirt with jeans.

36

"Hello Curtis," she said warmly as she hugged him back. Since Keith's death, her hugs were always a little tighter. "How's my handsome son?" she asked as she smiled and brushed his hair back with her hand. It was something she always did to both him and his brother when they were growing up. It made him grimace and smile all at the same time. "You hungry? Why don't you get a plate, and we can sit and have some breakfast?" Once they were all seated with full plates, he began to tell his parents about last night. His mom put her hand on her chest and said, "That poor girl. I always remember Florence's sister as such a sweet girl. I hate that she will have this horrible memory the rest of her life."

He glanced up at his dad, who usually was the calm one and the rock of the family. He had fire in his eyes, "I'm glad you were there. What happened to the bastard who did this?" Owen looked at his son and asked, "What happened to your hand?"

He looked at his parents, "Well, I had my rifle aimed at him and had to get Karen to move over by me so she would be safe. Then the police came into the building and told me to lower my rifle."

His dad asked, "Well, how does that explain your hand being bandaged?"

"Let's just say the SOB won't be able to breathe too well for a while. I broke his nose after he said something demeaning about her. I really don't like rude people, especially assholes who abuse women."

His father gripped his son's shoulder and said, "That's my boy." His dad cleared his throat, "About the glass door at the coffee shop…"

"Already taken care of Dad. The owner said she had insurance and not to bother, but I told her it was something I wanted to do since Karen enjoys working there. I just thought it would be helpful to replace the door."

Abby looked at her husband, "So, I guess we did a good job after all raising these kids." She asked, "How is Karen?" He told his parents about the hospital visit last night and meeting with the detective.

His dad said, "When you find out, let me know who the asshole is so I can contact our lawyer if need be."

"I already put a call in to Chuck, Dad. He said he's going to ask the detective working the case for a copy of the police report."

Owen Dalton looked at his wife with a twinkle in his eye, "Well, Hon, looks like our children don't need us anymore. Maybe we should sell the house and the farm and move into a condo in Orange Beach. What do you think of that idea? We could hang out in our beachwear and flip flops drinking beer and wine."

She looked at her husband with a knowing smile, "Well, if I can get these stubborn pounds off, I can get back into that bikini I used to wear when the children were small. That way when we go to the beach, your eyes won't be drifting to look at all those 30-something year olds in what I call their "barely there" suits."

His dad raised his eyebrows and smiled. Owen got up from his chair, walked to his wife and pulled her into his arms, "Abby, my dear," he grinned, "if we can move our son here along, I can show you how I only have eyes for you." Then he kissed her.

Curtis knew when he was in the way, "Okay, you two, get a room." He smiled at them and said he was leaving.

Abby hugged her husband and remarked, "Hang on, Curtis." She ducked into the living room. While waiting on his mom, he cleared his place at the table. She returned holding a stack of magazines, "If you do happen to check on her, maybe she would like to have these. There's a variety there." His mom held sadness in her eyes, "Maybe it will take her mind off what happened just for a little while." Owen put his arm around his wife.

"Thanks, mom. I'm sure she'll appreciate it." He waved to his parents who were holding on to each other. That's how he always remembered them growing up. As the door closed behind him, he hoped that one day he could find what they had. He sat in his truck and his thoughts turned to Karen. He looked across at the magazines on his front seat. He hadn't heard from her today and texted Florence to see how she was feeling. She replied that it was rough at her mom's house. She had stayed the night with them. Karen hadn't slept and wouldn't eat anything. He thanked Florence for the information. He saved her number to his contacts and called her.

"Hello?" asked Karen cautiously.

"Hi, it's me, Curtis. I just called to check on you," There was silence on the phone, "Karen?"

"I don't really feel like talking right now."

He heard a catch in her voice. His heart plummeted, but he just plowed ahead, "Would you mind if I come for a visit? I just want to drop something off to you." He waited.

"Sure. You'll be over soon?"

"Yes. I have one errand to run and then I'll be right over." She hung up the phone. Curtis realized he wanted to help her. He remembered how happy she was that morning in the coffee shop when she made him a special blend of coffee. Such a little thing, but it made her happy. He wanted to see her happy again. He glanced up to heaven. It was one of those beautiful Alabama mornings when the sun was out and there was nothing but stretches of blue sky as far as the eye could see, "Keith, I hope I'm doing the right thing." He sighed, "It would also be nice if you gave me a sign or something, so I know you're listening." He smiled to himself. He got into his truck and turned on the radio. Keith's favorite country song was on the air. He leaned back in his seat and grinned, "Thanks man."

Chapter 5

Curtis pulled up at the Smiths' house. He remembered coming over with Keith when Florence had visited her family here. The neighborhood had been established in an older area called Midtown. Trees lined the sidewalks. It was a pretty neighborhood. Houses had been given fresh coats of paint and the lawns were meticulous. Getting out of his truck, he peered at the "For Sale" sign on the front lawn. He jogged up the steps carrying the stack of magazines and rang the doorbell.

Janet greeted him at the door with a smile that didn't quite reach her eyes, "Hello, Curtis. She's waiting for you on the back porch." Janet shifted her stance and told him, "It's been rough for her." Janet had tears in her eyes, "I just want to thank you. I don't know what would have happened if you hadn't intervened. She can't sleep. I can't get her to eat anything. Whatever you can do to bring her some peace, I would be so grateful." Her mom looked at the stack of magazines, "Oh, you're so kind to bring those over for her." She touched his arm, "Your parents raised good boys. We miss Keith," She gave him a small smile.

"Yes ma'am. I miss him too."

She pointed to the door to the back porch, "Please let me know if you need anything. I'm going to be cleaning out some things. You all have a nice talk." She walked out of the room.

Taking a deep and steady breath, Curtis opened the door to the back porch and said, "Hi."

She was dressed comfortably in a t-shirt and leggings and was ensconced in a wicker rocking chair. She was seated hugging her knees with her chin resting on top of them. He was careful to show no reaction to the haunted look in her eyes. The bruise on her face was even more pronounced today. There was a wooden bench surrounded by a garden of flowers that was situated in such a way that allowed him to face her when he took a seat. He laid the magazines on the bench beside him, "I brought some magazines with me from the farm just in case you wanted something to read."

She eyed the magazines, "Thank you." She cleared her throat, "I will always be grateful for what you did for me. I just don't want you to feel you have to come over here to keep me occupied, feel sorry for me, or feel obligated to help me any further with...." Karen teared up and couldn't finish her thoughts.

"Can I be honest with you?" he asked. She nodded her head. "I'm not here because I feel sorry for you. I'm angrier than anything. I'm concerned for you because I know that asshole is still out there. I could be wrong, but I think that has to consume your thoughts." She looked at him and hugged her knees tighter to her chest. He continued, "I want to help." He hated this for her. He hated the uncertainty she was feeling. He wanted justice for her, but he was realistic enough to know the wheels of justice turned slowly for those who were victims. Curtis leaned forward, "I don't know if it's right to say this, but I'm only going to say it to you, and I'm only going to say it once." She peered at him with questioning eyes, "If I could have ended things that night for you, I would have. Then you wouldn't have to look over your shoulder or worry that he'll show up again. If he had come at me or you again, I wouldn't have hesitated. I was taught to defend myself and to protect others." He cleared his throat and felt his eyes moisten. He moved from the bench and knelt down in front of her chair, "I'm so sorry I wasn't there earlier to stop it from happening. If I could do anything to turn back the clock I would. I just want you safe and I want him locked up."

She locked eyes with him, "I don't want him locked up. I want him dead. Is that wrong to say?"

He gently touched her hand and shook his head, "No, not at all. Peace never comes easy for those who need it the most."

She put her hand in his and said, "I think we understand each other, don't we?"

He inclined his head in agreement. He stood up, put his hands in his pockets and looked around her backyard,

"You've got a nice garden growing here. Do you mind if I look around?"

Feeling more settled with him there she said, "I don't mind. I'll walk with you." Janet was walking through the living room with a basket of laundry and looked out the back window. She stopped and watched the scene unfold. Her baby girl was talking to Curtis as she showed him around the garden and flower beds. Janet hoped this was one small step for her daughter to heal. Her family had gone through enough trauma to last them a lifetime. Florence was happily married. Edward and she were engaged. It was now time for her youngest to have true happiness in her life. Maybe it would be with a career. Maybe it would be with a soul mate, or maybe she could have it all. She just wanted her to be happy. Janet didn't think that was asking too much at all.

Curtis leaned on one of the trees in the backyard. He surveyed the yard and noticed a hammock tucked in the corner, a few benches for taking in the view of the garden and flowers and even a small fountain surrounded by monkey grass. Karen told him her mom put a lot of time and effort into the yard. It showed. His eyes tracked her as she picked flowers. She told him she needed a bouquet to put on the picnic table closest to the backdoor. Even in sadness and pain, she had a quality about her that made him want to take care of her. He knew there was an underlying toughness there. She wasn't in bed with the covers over her head or confining herself to her room. She had gotten up this morning, gotten dressed and made her way to sit in a chair outside. He watched as she finished picking flowers and joined him at the tree. He couldn't help but notice how pretty she was with her green eyes and long brown hair, "That's a nice collection of flowers."

She peered at Curtis leaning on the tree. She learned in the short time she had known him that he was patient, kind and protective. Those were not his only qualities she admired. She had noticed more than once how handsome he was with his eyes a warm shade of brown and how strong he felt when he held her at the hospital. The conversation they had this morning made her feel a little closer to him. That didn't mean they were going to start a relationship or anything, far from it at this point. But it was nice to have someone to lean on who understood her. They walked over to the picnic table. Karen arranged the flowers in a vase while he took a seat at the table and watched her. She sat beside him and admired her handiwork. He spoke, "The colors remind me of a few fields of wildflowers we have bordering one of the roads through the farm. Even though they look like they take care of themselves, it takes a lot of work to keep them growing."

She joined in, "It must be a lot of work to take care of your family farm."

"Yes, sometimes it feels like it's a 24/7 job and I'm not getting any younger." He smiled.

He was so surprised when she bumped his shoulder with hers and said, "You're not so old. You seem to have all your own teeth and you look like you're in pretty good shape. What are you, like 40?" Her eyes twinkled when she looked at him.

He bumped her shoulder back and said, "That's not funny." But he was smiling inside. He was glad she was talking with him and even letting some of that light out that she always seemed to radiate.

"Yeah, it is. Isn't that the age you get those senior citizen envelopes in the mail for food discounts?" Karen asked as she wrinkled her nose and smiled.

He played along, "Yes, I was going to ask you out to dinner, but we'd have to be there at 4:00 so we can get a good seat."

"Don't let my mom hear you say that. She and Ed go out to eat early sometimes. I couldn't begin to think about going to dinner that early." They both laughed. He was so glad to hear her laughter.

"Actually," Curtis remarked, "would you be interested in going out with me to get an ice cream?"

She looked at her watch, "You do know it's almost lunch time?"

"So? You never ate dessert and ruined a meal? When we were young, Keith and I snuck into the kitchen and ate about 6 brownies off a dessert tray mom had made for a bake sale for school the next day. She had even put a note on it that said it was for the school and no touching. Mom knew what we had done and made us eat our whole dinner even though we weren't hungry. It was vegetable night and mom made cauliflower and broccoli. Keith and I were so sick. We took turns running to the bathroom."

He smiled at the memory. She propped her chin on her hand and looked at him. "The next day when we woke up, we were so nauseous. When we got to the kitchen, Mom made a huge breakfast and asked if we were hungry. Turns out she had to get up early to bake more brownies. She smiled at us. Keith and I just looked at each other and put our heads on the table. We never did that again as tempted as we were since Mom baked a lot for other people."

"Your mom's a good person. When we would visit, she always had treats for us and took time to talk to us. Your mom always had a smile on her face."

He said, "Don't let that smile fool you. She would let us know quickly if she wasn't happy with us. Of course, all Dad had to do was look at us and we'd straighten up. Mom would get quiet if we did something obnoxious. We felt so bad because we'd hurt her feelings by not listening, especially Keith. He was the baby and hated to hurt Mom's feelings. He had a big heart." Curtis got quiet and folded his hands on the table.

She put her hand on top of his, "I think you have a big heart too. You didn't have to come back that night to check on me at the coffee shop, but you did." He turned his head and met her eyes, which were full of tears, "I'm so glad you were there."

He turned his hand over and held her hand in his, "I hate that you have that memory. You're a kind person. You didn't deserve what he did to you." He paused, "But there are a lot of people around you who care about you and want to replace those bad memories with good ones."

Karen was quiet. She looked at him, "Ice cream, huh?"

He grinned, "I'm now thinking about lunch. I'm starving. I know a little sandwich place that overlooks the bay. We could sit on the back deck. It wouldn't be busy if we got there before noon. What do you say?"

She let his hand go and hugged herself. She looked back at him. He was such a nice man and had been a good friend to Florence, "Okay." Karen went in to talk to her mom. Curtis arrived in the living room and waited. She and her mom appeared from the back room. She hugged her mom. Janet Smith smiled at him and nodded.

They walked to the truck and he held the door open for her. She thanked him. As Curtis started the engine, he waited. Karen turned his way, "Something wrong?" He sighed, leaned over into the back seat, and pulled out a gift bag. She gave him a puzzled look. She opened the bag and pulled out a hat, "You got me a JAGS hat!" She put on the hat and said, "I don't have this one!" Before she could think she reached across the seat and gave him a big hug. He touched her arm and when she pulled back, she was grinning at him, "Thank you so much!" He cleared his throat and tried not to think of her softness and the scent of her when she hugged him. He gazed at her pretty green eyes and told her she was welcome.

Karen had pulled the mirror down on the sun visor,

"Curtis Dalton, I look pretty good in this JAGS hat, don't I?"

He sighed at the hat but could only tell her the truth about her beauty, "Yeah, you do." Curtis exhaled and drove away.

She finished her turkey sandwich and looked at the view of the bay. It was a cool, but sunny day for November. Curtis was watching Karen and hoping that this time outside was helpful. He was pleased to see that she did eat her sandwich. She continued to look over the water, "Curtis, it's okay. I'm not going to starve myself. I know my mom worries. I want to thank you for taking me here." She glanced his way, "I promise you, I'm not being rude, but can we just sit in silence and look at the water? It's comforting."

He nodded and hoped she could find peace. After leaving the restaurant and seeing how much the bay calmed her, he drove her home via the Causeway route. She was mesmerized by the water but didn't spot any alligators. She usually would see one or two in the summer, but this time of year there were none visible. The events the night before had taken a toll on her. With the sun making the interior of the truck warm and being full from lunch, she drifted off to sleep.

He looked over to see that Karen had fallen asleep. She must be exhausted. He turned on some soft music and shifted lanes to turn onto the access road to the Bayway so she could rest longer. Curtis's phone buzzed. He saw

Florence's number flash up on the screen, "Hey," he answered as he looked over at Karen. She was fast asleep, "Yes, she had a sandwich. We sat for a while at the restaurant." He explained that Karen was content to linger while at lunch and watch the water and now he was driving her home.

Florence asked him if she could talk to her, "Hon, she's fallen asleep, and I hate to wake her. Your mom told me she didn't sleep last night." Curtis looked over at her. She was in a deep sleep, "Yes, I'll let her know you called." Florence thanked him for checking on Karen and taking her to lunch, "Anytime."

As Curtis ended the call, he turned his head to check on his passenger. She shifted in her seat and her head landed on his shoulder. He moved in his seat slightly so she could be more comfortable. As he drove, he realized he liked the feeling of having her count on him, even for a short time, to make things a little better for her.

Karen's eyes gradually opened. She realized the truck had stopped and that her head was on his shoulder. His warm brown eyes met hers. She sat up and said, "I'm so sorry to have fallen asleep on you."

"It's okay. I'll probably get feeling back in this arm in a few months," he smiled.

A small smile surfaced on her face and lit up her eyes. Her smile was breathtaking, he thought. "I guess I was more tired than I thought. I really haven't slept." A shadow moved across her eyes.

Curtis put his hand on hers, "It's okay. I took the long way so you could rest."

"You're so kind. I appreciate it."

"Hang on and I'll get your door." He came around the truck and opened her door. She gathered her bag. As she gazed at his kind eyes, she thanked him once again for her day out. Curtis told her if she needed him, just to give him a call and he would check on her again.

Her mom opened the front door for them and saw the bag and hat, "Mom, thanks to Curtis, I have one more hat for my collection."

Janet's eyes moistened, "Thank you."

"Yes ma'am." He looked at Karen and said, "Since I had to let that hat sit in my truck, I'll collect on that ice cream next time." He winked at her and was glad to see the smile on her face. He said his goodbyes and headed to his truck.

Love from Farm to Stable

Chapter 6

Clarence Higgins III was sitting at his country club nursing his scotch and soda. He was so bored. His dad had set up a dinner with a prominent family who had a daughter about his age, but he wasn't interested in marriage. Of course, if it meant keeping his financial status, he would do what was necessary. Dear Old Dad started putting on the pressure and talking about cutting off his money supply. Clarence wasn't about to let that happen. He thought out loud, "I can do anything I want. I'm Clarence Higgins and I always get everything!" His dad said he should have never messed with someone connected with the Daltons. They could make life uncomfortable for him. Some skirt teaser wasn't going to make him lose what he worked so hard to keep. He had to admit to himself that she was all he could think about. Karen Smith. He remembered how she smelled like flowers and how she played hard to get.

So, she was trying to get away and he had to hit her. That's what you do with women who wouldn't listen. Clarence learned that from the cradle. When his mother fought back his dad backhanded her and had security that made sure she never left the house. When she threatened to tell anyone who would listen, he had her put in a psychiatric facility with around the clock guards. She had been released to her family years ago because they were considered an American dynasty with Presidents and high-powered people counted as friends. So, she didn't stay there long. Her family had ceased all contact with him and his dad. Annoyance clouded his expression. Good riddance. Simpering females weren't his cup of tea. His thoughts returned to his quest of Karen Smith. Clarence was going to have her one way or another. He knew somebody that might help. An old liaison who never quite got over losing her golden goose, Curtis Dalton.

Sunny during the day and cool at night was the forecast for this week. On Thursday afternoon, Curtis surveyed his cotton fields that had been planted in the spring. It was always amazing to him to know planting something a certain time of the year would yield crops several months later. Some crops should be rotated such as peanuts and cotton. Farming was a hard profession, weather determined when to grow and some equipment was more expensive than some waterfront homes. Land prices had skyrocketed, and many farmers were selling out. Farming was a lot different now than in his grandparents' day. As frustrating as it was, Curtis had grown to love it. He just wished his brother was alive to share the good with the bad of running a farm. His family was truly fortunate that their farm was a success. It took a lot of hard work that continued from one generation to the next.

Curtis leaned on his truck. He often came out here to think. Swirls of blue, orange, and yellow filled the sky as the sun was on its way to sleep. The sunsets in Alabama couldn't be beat. He was comfortable with his own company but wouldn't mind having someone to share this view. At times, he was lonely. Thoughts of Karen came to mind. They had talked a few times this week. He was surprised the first time she called him. The conversation centered mostly around topics such as the park where her sister worked, the latest additions to her mom's garden or being peppered with questions about his family farm. There was never any talk about her next step, which he thought might be counseling related to the incident at the coffee shop. He kept the conversation light and answered her questions about life on the farm. One of these days he should ask her if she'd like to come for a visit. He couldn't remember the last time she was here. Probably right before Keith's death. His brother was always good about letting Karen tag along when he brought Florence to the farm.

He sighed as the sunset or what he liked to call the "ball of fire" finally settled down and disappeared so that night could take over the sky. Tomorrow would be Friday. Another day on the farm. He sighed. When night fell, he would either retreat to his home to watch TV or have dinner at his parents' house. He was in a rut, but he didn't have to be. He reached in his back pocket for his phone and knew just who to call.

Friday night, Karen gazed at her companion in the SUV. She was so glad when Curtis called to ask if she would like to see a movie. She had enough of confining herself to the house. There was a showing of Rear Window at the Quarter Moon Theater in Downtown Mobile. Curtis told her it was one of his family's favorite movies. She would be seeing this movie for the first time. He looked nice in his blue checkered button down, jeans and boots. A hint of a five o'clock shadow only intensified his ruggedness. "You keep staring at me like that, and I'll start to wonder if I have something on my face, if I forgot to shave or my clothes don't match."

Her face heated, and she turned her head to look out of the window, "No, you look fine." That was an understatement she thought. He looked more than fine.

When he picked Karen up at her house, she had sauntered down the steps in a pair of black jeans, a white t-shirt and a black leather jacket. She wore her hair loose so that it cascaded down her back. He had no business thinking how good she looked in those jeans or how sexy she was in her leather jacket. He slowed down to let a crowd of people pass on the downtown street. Curtis glanced her way. His eyes took in the long brown hair, the contour of her face and the fun of the gold earrings that dangled from her ears. The bruise on her face had faded. He was glad she wouldn't have that reminder much longer when she looked in the mirror each day. "You keep staring at me and you'll make me think I have something on my face, if I forgot to put on makeup or if my clothes don't match," she turned her head and met his gaze.

His mouth turned up. She smiled. "Sassy. That was very sassy," he remarked.

"Something wrong with being sassy?"

"No ma'am. It looks good on you." he said as his gaze traveled from her eyes to her lips. She blushed and he grinned. He drove ahead and pulled over into a parking spot not far from the theater. Curtis grabbed his jacket and headed to the other side to open her door.

"Thank you." She was close enough to him to notice his cologne. He smelled so good, she thought.

He caught a whiff of her light floral scent and thought she smelled amazing, "You're welcome." As they walked to the theater, Karen watched the crowds taking in the buzz of the nightlife downtown. Families were dining together in many different restaurants. College students were spilling out of the bars with to-go cups. Couples were walking arm in arm. The city had strung lights up overhead so when walking down the street it made her feel as if Christmas had arrived. At one point, he put his hand lightly on her back to help steer her through crowds. She realized she liked his touch; it made her feel safe. Curtis opened the door to the theater. It turned out to be a small place. Karen took in the movie posters pinned to the walls, the wonderful aroma coming from the popcorn machine and the selection of wine, beer and sodas. He asked her if she would like anything.

"We could share the popcorn if you don't mind. I just want a little. A glass of wine would be nice," she responded. He handed her the popcorn as he carried his beer and her wine. Karen made her way to the back of the theater to two seats available on the far end of a row. She looked back at Curtis and he nodded his head. As they got settled, he brushed her fingers when handing her the wine. She took a slight breath and looked at him, "Thank you." His eyes took in her slightly flustered look. He took a deep breath of his own and took a sip of his beer.

The lights went out and the picture rolled onto the screen. She watched as Grace Kelly played the role of Lisa and Jimmy Stewart was Jeff. They bantered back and forth throughout the movie and were good together. She reached for some popcorn and met his hand reaching into the bag, "Sorry," she said.

"Not a problem," he replied. Munching on popcorn and watching a movie next to Curtis was a highlight compared to the last two weeks of her life. There was something so comforting about him. She watched as he smiled at a funny line delivered by Jimmy Stewart's nurse. She settled back in her seat and sipped her wine. She loved watching all the different neighbors that the character Jeff could see through his rear window in the movie.

Towards the end of the movie, Curtis felt Karen's tension and noticed her stillness. He looked up at the screen and cursed himself. It was a scene in which Grace Kelly's character was discovered in the apartment by the man whom she suspected had killed his wife. The man

58

was trying to choke her. Curtis entwined his fingers with hers. She held on to his hand in a firm grip. The scene ended with the police rescuing the woman. As the villain in the movie made his way to Jimmy Stewart's apartment, a fight ensued on screen. Karen's fingers tightened. He switched out his hand and put his arm around her shoulders. The police detective and his crew caught up with the man just as Jimmy Stewart's character fell out of the window but was caught by two policemen. As the ending credits rolled on the screen, people emptied out of the theater. Curtis turned to Karen and touched her cheek, "I'm so sorry. I didn't think."

She put her other hand on top of his, "It's just a movie. I can't react this way the rest of my life and I can't have those bad memories overtake the good ones. Being here with you tonight is a good memory. I want to thank you for that." She squeezed his hand and let it go.

"I enjoyed being here with you too." He removed his arm from the back of her seat. He had noticed the cleaning crew come in to get the room ready for the next showing, "Ready?" She nodded her head.

As they threw away their trash on the way out, she asked Curtis, "Do you think we could take a walk? It's a beautiful night and I'd like to walk under the lights hanging over the street." Curtis could see the street had been blocked off so that people could use the street for walking. He held out his arm and she placed her hand there.

He was content to stroll with her in silence as they glimpsed a bar with dueling pianists singing and taking requests from patrons. A high school football game was being shown on a big screen TV outside one of the bars and people were lined up at a food truck serving beignets. It was a lively scene and fun just to be a spectator. He stopped at an outside bar stand and looked at Karen. She shook her head. He purchased two bottles of water and handed her one. They wandered past a candy shop. The window display offered many different glass containers filled with nuts and a variety of candies for sale. During their walk, she discovered loft apartments with people sitting on their balconies enjoying the night air. They made their way to the other side of the street and headed back to the SUV.

She was walking on the inside closest to the buildings when a blonde-haired older businessman came out a side door and bumped right into her, "Miss, I'm sorry," he said as he held her arm to steady her. Karen's eyes went wide as she reached for Curtis. He pulled her into his arms. The man let go of her, "Miss, are you okay?"

Karen couldn't breathe, "Curtis," was all she could get out.

"I'm here." He told the man things were fine. The man stared at them and went on his way.

"Curtis?"

"Let's get you in the car, okay? It's not him. It's not him." She took a deep breath and let him guide her to the car. He opened her door and made sure she was safely buckled before he made his way to his door. Once inside his SUV, he locked the doors and turned to her, "Hey, I'm right here." Tears were in her eyes. She unbuckled her seatbelt and inched across the seat until she was holding him. He held her and smoothed his hand down her hair, "I've got you." He kissed the top of her head, and she held him tighter.

She then leaned back slightly to look at him and she wiped her eyes. He brushed the hair out of her face as her voice hitched on a sob, "I'm sorry. I'm so sorry."

He noticed she was beginning to take easier breaths, "Karen, I want you to remember that you don't ever have to apologize to me when it comes to this." He put his hand on her cheek. Her eyes met his. He leaned forward slowly until his lips touched hers. Her lips parted and she kissed him back. Curtis shifted his hands to cup the back of her head, and he deepened the kiss. Karen had never experienced the sensations she was feeling with anyone else. She trusted him. His lips roamed from her mouth to her cheek and his hands settled on her shoulders. Slowly, he leaned back. She could see his eyes filled with desire and longing, which he quickly shuttered. "Karen, I um..." He cleared his throat and tried again, "I didn't mean for that to happen. I'm sorry."

"You just told me I didn't have to apologize for how I acted tonight. It's a two-way street with us, okay?" She held his hands, "I'm not sorry it happened." Her eyes captured his, "I liked it."

He sucked in a breath and slowly moved back to his seat. Karen inched back into her seat and buckled her seat belt. They turned to each other and he said, "I liked it too." Then he started the car, put his blinker on and merged into traffic.

Chapter 7

Saturday began the day with a storm. Karen turned over and pulled the covers up. She was going to linger in bed this morning. It was still early. Thoughts of last night filled her head. When Curtis walked her to the door, he kept his hands in his pockets, but his eyes told another story. As he waited for her to go in, Karen was quietly opening the door so not to wake her mom. As she had her back to the door holding onto the knob, a slow smile lit up her face and reached her eyes. His eyes showed a tender expression, and a slow rolling grin transformed his face as he wished her goodnight. She slept peacefully last night for the first time since the incident in the coffee shop. Karen had him to thank for that. She was so happy that she couldn't stay in bed for long.

She'd surprise her mom with breakfast. Fifteen minutes later bacon was sizzling in the pan, biscuits were fresh out of the oven and eggs were scrambled. Karen was just finishing up the coffee when her mom walked into the room. "Well, what's all this?" Janet asked. Karen hugged her mom as Janet kissed her on the cheek. Her mother took in the smile and her happy mood.

"I couldn't sleep any longer and decided to make you breakfast. A daughter can't give back to her mom for once?" Karen smiled and handed her mom a cup of her special blend of coffee with cinnamon and nutmeg.

Janet took a sip and sighed, "Honey, you could make a fortune just making coffee. It's terrific."

"Is Ed around this morning?" asked Karen.

"No, honey. He had an early trip this morning to the shooting range." Karen fixed two plates and joined her mother at the table, "Thank you. How was the movie last night?"

She told her mom she was enjoying the movie until a scene made her anxious and Curtis was so sweet to hold her hand to get her through, "We walked around after the movie. There were so many people downtown. I forgot how much there is to see and do down there." Karen got quiet.

Janet was sipping her coffee when she noticed the quietness and looked over at her daughter. She reached for Karen's hand, "Tell me what happened. Something is bothering you."

"We were walking back to the car and a man came out from his office and bumped into me. He looked just like the man who attacked me at the shop. I couldn't catch my breath. I reached for Curtis and he pulled me away from the man."

"Oh, Karen."

"It's okay. It wasn't him. Curtis got me back to the car and told me I was safe, and it was going to be okay. I apologized for acting the way I did. He told me I had nothing to be sorry for and he was right there to help me." Of course, she didn't share with her mom about her kiss with Curtis. She smiled inwardly at the memory.

Janet said, "Curtis is a good person. I have always liked his family."

Karen smiled, "He talks about them and they seem very close. Despite what happened, I enjoyed going out last night." Karen paused and looked at her mother, "You know, Mom, that has me thinking. I've been getting out a bit lately. You know how my boss has been keeping in touch with me. I might see if I could start back gradually at work. She's hired a security guard and she's redecorated the shop so maybe the memories of that night won't be so bad."

Worry filled her mother's face, "Do you think that's a good idea? Did you talk to Florence about it?"

"I haven't. I thought I might make this decision on my own. I just might need some support. Maybe you can take me there if you have time once I talk to my boss."

Her mom responded, "I can do that. I'm proud of you." She got up to hug her daughter, "Thank you for breakfast. I'll clean up if you want to call your boss."

Karen took a deep breath and dialed the number. By noon that day, she had worked everything out with her boss. She was nervous, but really missed seeing her customers at the coffee shop. Her boss even told her they asked about her and she told them she was under the weather. Karen called Florence to tell her the news. Her sister was concerned but would support her. She spent the better part of the afternoon helping her mom clean the house. She'd been charging her phone when she heard it buzz. She looked at it and realized she had received a text. It was from Curtis.

"Hi,"

Karen grinned. She texted back, *"Hi yourself."*

"How are you today?"

"I'm good. For the first time since that night in the coffee shop, I slept all night."

"That's great. I'm glad."

"Thank you for last night."

"Which part? "he asked.

Karen was so happy texting with him she thought she'd throw him a curve ball,

"The part where you asked me to run away with you and live in sin for the rest of our lives."

"Excuse me?"

"Oh, this isn't Tom? I'm sorry. I must be texting with the wrong person. Oops."

"That's not funny."

Karen laughed. *"Yeah, it is. I would love to see your face about now."*

"How'd you like to see my face tomorrow afternoon? I thought we could take a drive and walk on the beach."

She told him she was planning to go back to work tomorrow morning just for a couple of hours, but she would be available tomorrow afternoon.

"I would love to go for a drive."

"Are you ready to go back to work so soon?" he texted.

"I can't hide forever. I'm ready to live again."

"If you want to talk at any time in the morning, all you have to do is call me. I'm here for you."

She was all smiles, *"Thank you, Curtis.*

They made arrangements for tomorrow afternoon.

"You have a good night. Sleep well."

"I will. See you tomorrow and thanks again."

"Anytime." he responded.

Sunday came sooner than expected for Karen. Florence showed up bright and early with some of Aunt Alice's apple and blueberry muffins. Florence drank a cup of her special blend and enjoyed a muffin as well, "I thought I would drive you all to the coffee shop. It would give us girls a chance to catch up." Karen looked at her sister across the table. Florence saw the worry in her sister's eyes. "Hey, you can always try this another time."

Karen shook her head, "I need to do this, Flo."

"Okay." Florence cleared the table as her mom came into the room.

"You girls ready?" asked their mom and then she hugged her youngest daughter.

"Yes," Karen replied. She took a calming breath and walked out the door. She was ready to begin her life again.

An hour flew by at the *Good to the Last Drop* coffee shop and she had been busy with a long line of customers. Some were on their way to church or just dropped by to say hello. She was heartened by their sincerity. They were glad to have her back in the shop serving their favorite drinks. Florence and her mom had stayed for a while to make sure she felt comfortable being back where she had suffered such a terrible event.

Karen took in all the changes her boss had made and she met Candace Murphy. She was a petite woman with beautiful mahogany skin and very fit. Candace was the full-time security guard at the shop who would make her feel safe. She had her own desk with a placard propped there that said *"Accountant."* Her boss felt Candace's cover was perfect as she had been an accountant before moving into law enforcement. She wanted the customers to feel comfortable coming to the shop without someone in full police gear. Candace also made sure the employees were escorted to and from their cars.

So far, it had been a good morning. Karen was rounding out her second hour at the shop. She was making a special blend for two of her favorite customers, Mr. and Mrs. Jenkins. They were originally from New Orleans but had settled in Mobile. They drove over every weekend to ask for special blends which usually centered around their Carnival coffees. She turned and handed them over to-go cups of their popular Mystic Revelers blend, "It's good to see you both."

"Oh, honey," Mrs. Jenkins gushed, "You make the best coffee, and we are so glad to have you back, aren't we Elmer?" Mr. Jenkins gave her a gift bag and winked. Karen pulled out a pair of Mardi Gras beads with writing on the circular emblem attached to the beads that read, "Stay calm and keep the coffee hot!"

She laughed. She came around the counter to hug them both, "Thank you." They waved bye to Karen. She checked the tables to make sure everyone had what they needed and replaced the napkins and cleared dishes. She was straightening behind the counter when she heard the door open. She turned around, ready to serve her next customer.

"Hello Karen," said Abby Dalton.

"Hi!" Standing before her were the Daltons: Abby, Owen and Leslie. She was glad to see them but hid her feeling of disappointment not to see Curtis.

Leslie moved forward, "We were on our way to church and thought we'd treat ourselves."

Karen took their orders to go and asked them if they'd like to have a seat while they waited. She had the coffees almost ready when she heard someone clear his throat behind her. "I'll be right with you." She packed up the 3 to-go cups in a cup holder and turned to deliver them to the Daltons. She almost dropped the holder when she saw her next customer. He looked so good in a blue button-down dress shirt, red and blue tie with khaki pants. He was the best thing she'd seen all day.

"Hi there. Do you have time to make one more to go?" Curtis smiled at Karen.

"Yes, sir," She beamed, "Let me deliver these to some important customers and I'll be right with you."

"I'll be waiting," he winked at her. She blushed and took the coffees to his family.

As she came back to the counter, she said, "I didn't think you were with them today when they all came in together."

"I drove today so I was parking the car."

She settled at the counter and asked, "What'll it be? A special blend? Cappuccino? Espresso? A frozen coffee? A Mardi Gras coffee?" she smiled as she rattled off the list of their favorite coffees.

"You're cute, you know that?"

"I try," She sighed, "Okay, one cup of boring black coffee coming up." He grinned at her.

Leslie was enjoying her coffee when she noticed her brother grinning at Karen, "Um, Mom, Dad. Take a look." Owen and Abby saw their son engaging in a conversation with Karen. They were laughing, gesturing with their hands, and talking as she poured him a to-go cup of coffee. Their fingers brushed as she handed him his coffee and she blushed. He said something to her that caused her to laugh. Curtis smiled as he sipped his coffee. "My brother, Curtis Dalton, is flirting with Karen. When is the last time we saw him laughing and carrying on with a woman?"

Her dad's mouth quirked up and he said, "Hmmm." He looked at his wife, "Abby? I got nothing here."

Abby watched her son. Her heart turned over as she leaned towards her husband, "I think he's smitten." The family watched in amazement as Curtis came alive around Karen.

Leslie tasted her coffee then said, "I think my brother is going down from the look on his face." She looked at her parents, "Maybe you all will be planning a wedding by Christmas. Just think, you could have a grandchild by next year!" she laughed.

Abby replied, "You're really enjoying yourself, aren't you?" Leslie's eyes twinkled and Owen had a grin on his face. "Not you too?" Abby remarked, "You all think you can give me a chance to catch up?" She rose from her chair, "Let's go. It's time to go to church and pray."

The family walked over to Curtis to let him know they were ready. Karen thanked them for coming in and they thanked her for the coffee.

They were almost to the door when Curtis turned to Karen, "Pick you up at 2:00?" She nodded and waved goodbye. He turned to see his family staring at him, "What?"

Owen answered, "Nothing. Just seeing if you were coming with us." He headed to the car with a smile on his face. His sister was laughing, and his mother just sighed.

Curtis shook his head as he got into the driver's seat. He looked in his rearview mirror and saw they looked pleased with themselves, "Sometimes I just don't understand my own family." That caused Leslie to laugh. He pulled onto the street.

Love from Farm to Stable

Chapter 8

Curtis jogged up the steps to Karen's house at 2:00 in the afternoon. Karen opened the door. Gone was the nice dress shirt and khakis she had seen him in this morning. He had replaced his dress clothes with an AU t-shirt, khaki shorts and tennis shoes. Karen had on a university t-shirt and jean shorts. She had scooped up a sweatshirt from her room to bring with her in case it got cold.

He waited for her to lock up, "Is your mom home?"

"No, she and Ed went to a play in Gulf Shores. I told her I'd see her later because I wasn't sure what time we'd be home."

"No set time, really. Just thought we'd have a nice walk and maybe see the sunset." Curtis gazed at Karen, "That's okay with you?"

"Hmm hmm," she replied.

"How was the rest of your time at the coffee shop?"

"It was good. Candace walked me out to my car. I saw a lot of people today who came by to visit." They reached his truck. He opened her door.

He looked at her, "Did you now? Anyone I know?"

73

She peeked back at him, "Yes. There was a man that came in all dressed up for church. He was very handsome." She climbed into the truck.

"Handsome huh?" He smiled to himself as he waited to close Karen's door.

"I even remember what he ordered, a black coffee."

"Really?"

"Yes, he came in right before you did," her eyes twinkled with laughter.

He closed her door and went around to get in on his side. As he got settled, he turned to make a smart remark, but got distracted by her laughter. His gaze travelled from her mouth curved in happiness to her pretty green eyes and back again to her mouth. His eyes met hers. The laughter in her eyes was replaced by awareness of him. At the moment his warm brown eyes focused on her, she caught her breath and leaned towards him. He met her halfway, the tension in the truck felt by them both. Karen put her hand on his arm and touched her lips to his. He softly returned her kiss, enjoying the feel of her mouth on his. She put her hands on either side of his face as she ended the kiss. She saw desire in his eyes that matched her own. He took her hand and kissed her palm. Her breathing increased and her heart raced. He picked up her other hand and did the same, looking into her eyes. "Curtis?" she asked.

"Yes, Karen?"

She shifted in her seat to put her seatbelt on but was having trouble pulling it across as her hands were shaking. "Here, let me," he said. Curtis reached for the seatbelt and buckled it for her. He was so close that Karen could smell his cologne.

She took a deep breath, "I think we should head to the beach."

"Yes," he replied as he moved back into his seat, "That would be a good idea." Karen took in the scenery on the main highway as they travelled to the beach. They exchanged glances more than once on the drive. She had always thought of him as Florence's good friend, but they acted more like brother and sister. Karen never thought of Curtis as anything other than Keith's brother, until now. Her senses heightened when she was around him. She wanted nothing more than to touch him and be close to him. Karen thought he felt the same about her even though they had only been around each other for a brief time. He was older than her, but that didn't seem to matter now. She glanced his way, and a smile reached his eyes.

Curtis pulled his truck into the gravel parking lot next to the beach. There were only a handful of cars there. He opened her door and took her hand to help her out of the truck. He asked her if she would like a bottle of water as he had packed a cooler. She shook her head. As they headed onto the sand, his hand reached for hers. Hand in hand, they walked the beach and talked, discovering more about each other. Seagulls roamed the beach. Two dogs ran to the water's edge then back to their owners. Karen stopped from time to time to pick up a shell or two. As they rounded a bend, she spotted a concrete walkway with steps several feet from the water, "Think we can sit for a while?" she asked.

They sat on the steps. He pointed towards the water, "Look." Dolphins were rising from the water, plunging back under and surfacing once more. They watched boats filled with families pass by and wave. They waved back. As the sun lowered further in the sky, the lights from the gas rigs twinkled far from the shore. Karen marveled at the array of colors in the sky as the sun set. Blue merged with red and painted the sky with colors so magnificent, she had to blink and reached for his hand. They turned to each other. With the sun hidden and replaced by swirls of color in the sky, he leaned towards Karen and kissed her. She shivered as his mouth moved over hers.

"Are you cold? "Curtis asked.

"Not if you hold me."

"I think I can do that," he replied as he held her. He put his mouth on hers again and deepened the kiss. Screams of laughter from kids running down the beach broke them apart.

She took a deep breath as his lips left hers, "This is the nicest afternoon I've had in a long time," she told him.

Curtis soaked in her green eyes, her long brown hair, and the face he longed to continue touching. "Me too," he responded. Karen blushed. He smiled and he said, "Come on." They walked arm in arm as they headed back to his car. He held the door for her and asked her to sit with her feet pointed out the door. He used a towel to wipe the sand from her shoes and his before getting into the truck. He put the towel on the floor in the back and started the engine, "Are you hungry?"

"Yes. I wasn't hungry earlier, but now I'm starving."

"Being around water will do that to you. What would you like?" Karen pointed to a sign they passed advertising a seafood restaurant with a view. Curtis followed the sign and he turned into a restaurant overlooking the water. She pulled on her sweatshirt. He put his hand on her back as he followed her into the restaurant. She caught her breath at his touch. They requested a table by the window. The view was incredible. The sunset had turned to dusk. Curtis pulled out Karen's chair for her and he sat next to her.

The waitress provided menus for the table. Karen ordered a glass of wine and was promptly carded. She handed over her license as his eyes held amusement, "You only wish you looked as young as me."

He held his hands up in surrender, "I didn't say one word."

"You didn't have to. I can see it on your face."

He reached for her hand and asked, "What else do you see on my face?"

She saw humor turn to an intensiveness in his gaze, "Is that look for me? "she asked breathlessly.

"I want to be honest with you. I haven't dated anyone in a very long time. There's this routine of working for the farm, having dinner with my parents or keeping to myself in my house. Sure, there are many people I run into during the week. I go out every so often with a friend or two, but that's about it. Then you and I started going out as friends." Karen nodded. "Now what we have seems to be turning into something I don't think either one of us could have ever imagined."

"What are you saying?" she held her breath.

He shifted in his chair and said to her, "I'm 33 years old. I don't know what our families will think if we continue to go out together. I put off thinking about the age difference because I really enjoy our time together. I feel I can talk to you and you understand me. Karen, I've never had a companion who truly understands me. You're finishing college and beginning your new life once you graduate. You might be interested in seeing friends or guys your own age." He raised an eyebrow, "Do you really want to go out with someone my age? Doesn't that bother you at all?" he asked.

"Curtis, when I look at you, your age isn't important. Yes, it has crossed my mind. You saved me from a bad situation. Visiting my house, talking to me, treating me to gifts, taking me for drives and walks are all good things I look forward to now. These are things that make me feel close to you. I haven't had good experiences when it comes to men who have crossed my path in life. You know that." He nodded. The waitress delivered their drinks and took their orders. Once the menus were handed over, the waitress disappeared. Karen continued, "The few dates I've had were guys I knew from my college group who were really only friends. We went to the

78

movies and maybe a couple of college parties as a group. I was so busy studying and working that I really didn't have a lot of time for dating. There were a couple of guys my friends tried setting me up with, but they weren't interested in talking to me or what I wanted for the future."

She glanced at him, "They only had one goal in mind and that's not what I wanted at the time." His eyes narrowed. "It's okay. They never pushed the issue once they found out I wasn't interested. What I'm trying to say is that none of them opened a door for me, held my hand when I needed it or listened to what mattered to me. You, Curtis, have done all that for me." Karen swallowed and took a deep breath. She locked eyes with him and tightened her grip in his hand, "None of them made me feel even close to how you make me feel when you look at me, hold me or kiss me. You matter to me. I'd like to see you again."

Curtis squeezed her hand and said, "You matter to me too." Their food arrived. As bowls of gumbo were consumed and an order of crab claws was shared, they talked about her master's degree that will give her the tools to be a Speech Language Pathologist. Karen wanted to work with patients in a clinical setting to help them regain their speech after accidents or medical trauma.

He talked about improvements he wanted to add to the farm and talked about the many counties and states he travelled to on business. They shared stories about things they had encountered with their work and college. Karen told a story about a professor at the university who had asked her to deliver 36 coffees to his class before his students were about to take their board exams. One professor who taught her education class was from Chicago. He had ordered several deep-dish frozen pizzas from the pizza company in his hometown for his family every year and baked a couple for class one night. Curtis talked about the time he was out in the field for one of his classes at Auburn and a cow stepped on his foot. He was in pain for about a week. Karen laughed. He winced, but humor showed in his eyes, "At the time, it wasn't so funny. It hurt."

The waitress cleared their dishes and asked if they wanted dessert. Karen had a gleam in her eye as she looked at the dessert menu resting on their table. He followed her gaze to the picture of a piece of key lime pie. Karen asked, "Will you share a piece of pie with me? I couldn't possibly eat the whole slice."

He smiled and answered, "Sure." The waitress left to put in their order. "You have a real sweet tooth, don't you?" asked Curtis.

"Shh," Karen muttered, "If you say it out loud, then I have to remind myself how much I have to work out this week so these calories I'm about to consume won't show."

His eyes travelled slowly from her face and lingered on her shapely legs and back up again, "I don't think you have a thing to worry about."

Karen thought turnabout was fair play as she looked at his muscular shoulders and what she probably thought was washboard abs hiding under that t-shirt. He leaned on the table closer to her and asked, "Have you seen enough?"

She put her elbows flat on the table and leaned close enough to almost touch him, "Maybe. Then again, maybe not." She had a twinkle in her eyes.

The waitress arrived with their pie, "Here you go, folks. I brought an extra plate and silverware." She winked at them and moved to the next table. Karen cut the pie in half and gave Curtis his slice. She took a bite and closed her eyes as she savored the sweet lime flavor. A sigh escaped her. Her small slice was gone in seconds. She took a sip of water and realized Curtis wasn't touching his pie.

He smiled and slid his plate towards Karen, "Oh, Curtis, I couldn't. That's for you."

She pushed the plate back to him. "Karen Smith, I was just being polite. I'm not really a key lime pie guy. Go ahead," he pushed the plate back at her.

She stared into his eyes, which held laughter. "If you're sure," she said.

He nodded and couldn't help teasing her as he replied, "You know, they do sell whole pies here if you feel the need to take one home. Just think of a piece of pie calling your name at midnight. Then you could come work the farm with me tomorrow to erase any guilt you have about eating all that dessert."

She finished his slice, wiped her mouth with her napkin and replied, "Curtis Dalton, that was not very nice." She leaned forward, "You may have just forfeited your chance to walk me to my door tonight."

He put his hand over hers, "Well, we can't have that. That's the best part of a date." She glanced at him with a serious expression on her face. The waitress brought the check to the table and he settled the bill. Karen was quiet as he walked her to the truck and opened her door.

She turned to him and touched his arm, "Thank you for dinner."

He put his hand on hers, "Thank you for going to the beach with me." Curtis stood still while he waited for her to climb into the truck. Karen's eyes met his. She leaned forward and kissed him on the lips, "Just to let you know. You don't have to wait until you walk me to my door."

He put his hands on her shoulders, "That's good to know." He raised his hands to her face and brought her mouth to his. She returned his kiss. Curtis murmured, "You taste like key lime pie."

Karen leaned back and gazed at him, "Well, we better stop kissing since that's not your favorite dessert."

He returned her gaze, "I'll make an exception just this once."

She replied, "Oh, you will?"

"Hmm, hmm," uttered Curtis as he kissed her forehead, "ready to go?" She hugged him and nodded her head. He held her before helping her into the truck.

When he got into his seat, he started the engine then looked at her. She asked, "Everything okay?"

He picked up her hand and kissed it, "Couldn't be better." A smile reached her eyes as she settled in for the drive home.

Clarence was cursing that damn waiter at the restaurant. He had lost them. To his surprise, he had been sitting at the same seafood restaurant as Karen Smith and her sugar daddy. He'd been nursing a drink at the bar. They couldn't see him, but he certainly had a good view of them. From the way they were looking at each other, it looked like Farmer Boy was going to get some action tonight. Clarence thought it might be a good time to end things once and for all. He thought about the pistol he had hidden under his seat. All it took was one clean shot to the head and Karen was all his. He liked sex on the beach. He would make sure she liked it too.

He was sure she wouldn't let it go if he killed her boyfriend, so he'd have to make it look like a lover's spat. "Lots of sharks in the Gulf and no one would be the wiser," he muttered under his breath. As he paid his tab and sauntered out of the restaurant, he saw their truck pull off. He had lots of time. As he was walking to his car, a waiter ran out the door of the restaurant to give him his credit card he had left behind. Clarence had the truck in his sight when he had to stop for a red light. He couldn't run it because there was a damn cop sitting on the side of the road. "Shit!"

He saw the truck with about six cars in front of him. Clarence drove in anticipation. He had to take matters into his own hands since the person he thought would help him with Curtis Dalton was on an extended stay in Destin with some friends.

He looked ahead and couldn't believe his eyes. The truck had slowed down. As he started to accelerate, a car stopped suddenly in front of him, and he slammed on his brakes. There were cars to the left and right of him. He had nowhere to go. He hit his steering wheel, "Damn it!"
He finally made it to the intersection and turned right. He looked around, "Where'd you go, Curtis boy? I'm going to find you." Clarence drove up and down the street. He passed several waterfront homes. "Well, you're rich enough to have a beach house down here, Curtis, so let's see if I can find your truck."   After searching for 30 minutes, he realized he would have to try again another time. "Curtis, old boy, you better have a good time while it lasts. Karen Smith is going to be mine." He would finally pay him back for the broken nose and for taking what belonged to him.

Chapter 9

On Monday of Thanksgiving week Karen was working an early morning shift at the coffee shop. Candace was enjoying Karen's special blend, *Honey Almond Roasted Coffee,* and thinking how much she liked her job. Accounting had paid the bills at first, but then she'd lost interest in working for a big corporation. She had enough of what she needed put away in savings. It had been time for a career change, so she trained in law enforcement and belonged to a special division with security. Detective Myers had contacted her about this assignment, and she was glad he did. Candace looked up at Karen Smith. She liked her a lot. Karen was kind with a gentle nature and everyone who came through the door responded to her smile. She had a way with people.

Candace understood what almost happened to her in the shop. Detective Myers kept tabs on Clarence Higgins III. That was some serious money there, Candace thought, as she sipped on her coffee. But money or not, she was going to protect the employees of this shop. She had special training in firearms and was a crack marksman. Candace hoped it didn't come to that. This was a small shop, and it would be a shame if an innocent bystander was hit by a perpetrator's gun. She spotted Karen wiping down tables and noticed she looked especially happy today. She saw that she kept glancing at the door in between customers. Maybe she was hoping Curtis Dalton would pay her a visit. Even though Karen thought they were keeping it under wraps, she noticed how they stared at one another and how their hands touched when she handed him a coffee. She always blushed when he was around her. Candace smiled and looked back down at her paperwork. Her boss at the coffee shop asked her to look over some statements to see how she could improve her profits and Candace was happy to help.

Karen looked at the door for the third time. She really needed to get a grip as it wasn't likely he was coming in today. They both had jobs and she really didn't expect him to show up. But she could wish, as thoughts of last night made her smile. She pulled out her phone and saw a text had popped up. Karen felt the grin take over her face, "Candace, I'll be right out front for a few minutes, okay?"

The former accountant looked out the front window to see a truck parked by the door, "You take your time, honey." She smiled as she watched Karen open the door and fly into the arms of Curtis Dalton. "Well, well, well," she thought, "all is right with Karen's world." She looked down at her paperwork to give them some privacy.

He hugged her tight as she flew into his arms, "Well, hi yourself." He gazed into her happy eyes and put his hands on either side of her face. He kissed her and smiled, "Good morning."

"Good morning Curtis."

"I was on my way to Mobile and thought I'd stop by and try your special blend."

"Really?" she asked incredulously.

"Uh, no. Although I wouldn't mind a cup of black coffee to take with me on the road."

"Black coffee it is. Come on in," she smiled. He wiped his feet on the rug outside the door and followed her into the shop. He nodded at Candace and said hello. She nodded back and smiled at the two of them. If she wasn't mistaken, there were wedding bells in their future. They looked good together. As Karen poured Curtis a to-go cup, he thought she never looked more beautiful. Her hair was up in a bun and her pretty green eyes were sparkling. He was glad to see her happy and he hoped to see a lot more of what he liked to think of as her lightness. Even though he could spot the sadness underneath at times, she usually resonated joy. He was glad to be a part of her life and wanted things to stay that way. She handed him the cup and their hands brushed and lingered. As Curtis lifted his cup to sip his coffee, he winked at her and her mouth settled into a smile.

"Hmm, you could make angels weep. How you can make black coffee into something extraordinary, I'll never know. What's your secret?"

Karen had a mischievous look in her eyes, and she crooked her finger for him to move closer. She whispered, "I'm not telling you because if I told you the secret, then you'd just make it at home. You wouldn't come by here anymore for my coffee."

He moved closer and murmured, "You're smart enough to know I don't just come here for the coffee." Her quick grin lit up her whole face. He'd never get enough of looking at her beautiful face. Candace cleared her throat.

He stepped back, "Oh, here." He started to give her cash for the coffee.

She walked him to the door and shook her head, "Nope. Since you were so generous to provide dinner last night, this one's on me."

His mouth turned up and his eyes twinkled, "There's that sassiness." He swooped in for a quick kiss and waved goodbye to Candace. She stood at the door and watched him get into the truck. He started it and glanced at her. He left her with the image of an inviting smile as he drove away.

Candace joined her at the door, "I just have to say it honey. He is one sexy man."

Karen looked at Candace, bumped her shoulder and agreed, "Yeah, he is." They both sighed.

The rest of her day was busy. A second barista came in to help with the overflow of customers. It was that time of year when her boss took pre-orders for their famous cinnamon loaves. Thanksgiving would be here soon, and customers quickly depleted their supply of the sweet bread. Susie, the other barista, was in the back cleaning dishes as a customer walked out the door. Since Karen had no customers at the moment, she decided to clean the windows and the glass door. With that chore finished she took several cups to move them over to the shelf across the room. She glanced out the door at the moment when a blonde-haired older man in a black car drove slowly past the shop. He looked her way and winked. She dropped the coffee cups and they shattered on the floor. Candace quickly ran over just in time to see Karen staring at the back of a black car and quickly got out her phone and took a picture of the license plate. "Candace?" Karen called out.

"Hey, honey. I'm right here." The security guard took in the ceramic shards on the floor and called for Susie.

Susie came out from the back and noticed the broken cups on the floor, "I'll get a broom." She saw Karen was frozen staring out the window, "Karen?" Susie asked. Candace shook her head at the barista. She came back promptly and began to sweep.

"Karen, come on honey. Let's go sit down so Susie can sweep. We don't want you to step on anything sharp." With a blank expression on her face, she followed her to a table in the back. Candace pulled out a chair for her and gently sat her down. She pulled Karen's phone out of her apron pocket and dialed her sister, "Yes, it's Candace at the coffee shop. Can you get away? You're in town? Yes, she needs you. Your doctor friend wouldn't happen to be around, would he? You'll try to reach him? Yes, okay, bye."

The door opened and the next customer came to the counter to order a drink. Susie had cleaned the floor, "Be right with you." She washed her hands and served the customer a to-go cup. Fifteen minutes later, Florence rushed into the shop. Candace motioned for her to come to the back. Hunt made it there ten minutes later, carrying a medical bag. Susie had called the owner to let her know about Karen and she told her to place the Closed sign on the door and lock it.

Florence was sitting next to her sister and holding her hand. Karen was so still. Hunt knelt in front of her to shine a light in each eye. Karen focused on the light then blinked at Hunt, "There she is. Hey, Hon." Hunt went to place his hand on hers and she pulled it out of reach. He made sure his expression stayed neutral. Florence's eyes filled with tears.

Candace asked Susie to sit with Karen while she talked to Hunt and Florence. They made their way to stand by the front of the shop, "A black car drove by earlier. A man was in the car. Karen happened to be looking out the door as she was working inside here. That's when I moved up to the window and saw the car. I managed to get the license plate number and called it in. It's him." Florence's heart sunk.

Anger took over Hunt's usual good-natured expression and he asked, "What's being done? This is harassment."

90

"That's the hard part. He didn't come into the shop and he didn't do anything to threaten or harm her."

He ran his hand down his face, "If that's not the result of harm back there, I don't know what is. Hell, does he have to assault or physically hurt her for her to get some help from you all?" He saw the calm expression on Candace's face, "Sorry," he said.

"Not a problem. Detective Myers is working on a lead." She looked at Florence, "I would highly suggest the family move to another location for the time being. It wouldn't be unheard of for him to show up at her house, if he hasn't already. I'm betting he's cased the neighborhood and knows where your sister lives. He profiles as the type to do that. He's made his plan and now he's acting on that plan." She spoke to Florence. "I wanted to wait until you got here to see if you would call Mr. Dalton."

"Curtis?"

"Yes, that's him. Curtis Dalton. Since they are dating each other, I thought he'd want to know what happened." Florence and Hunt exchanged glances.

"Dating each other?" Florence asked.

"Yes, he's come by the shop a few times. They're a sweet couple. He dotes on her and treats her with such respect, which is heartening to see these days. She lights up every time they're together." Candace eyed Karen's sister, "You didn't know they were seeing each other? Maybe I shouldn't have said anything."

Florence managed to say, "It's okay. Yes, I needed to know so I could call him. You did the right thing in telling me."

Hunt touched Florence's arm, "I'm going to go check on Karen while you make that call." Candace and Hunt moved away.

Florence took a deep breath and dialed his number. She heard him pick up on the other end, "Curtis, I need to tell you something."

He hung up the phone. He was numb. According to Florence, Karen wasn't responding to anyone. Hunt felt there was nothing to gain from taking her to the hospital. He thought she needed to stay in familiar surroundings. Florence also made the comment since he was dating her sister, maybe Karen might do better responding to him. He didn't say anything when Florence said they'd discuss their relationship later. They'd have that conversation once Karen was better. They needed to focus on her for now. Florence told him about Candace's suggestion of moving the family. He told Florence he thought he could help with that. He would put in a call to get that set up and would call her back. Curtis dialed his father, "Dad, I need your help."

The Smith family arrived at the Dalton home. Abby and Owen were waiting on the porch. Abby walked down the steps and hugged Janet. "Thank you," said Janet, "we appreciate you opening one of your homes to us."

Owen walked down the steps to shake Edward's hand, "We're happy to help."

Owen and Abby saw Karen in the car. Abby asked Janet, "How is she?"

Karen's mom shook her head and tears started to fall. Abby put her arm around her shoulders. "She's quiet and won't talk to anyone. Is Curtis here? Maybe she'll open up to him. He always seems to know just what to say to her and she's always happier when he's around." Janet took a breath and glanced at their car, "I think we might need to have a talk, though, about them seeing each other."

Abby and Owen looked at each other, "They've been going out a lot?" Abby asked.

Janet said, "Oh, here and there. He took her out to lunch one day, to the movies one night and they went for a walk on the beach yesterday afternoon. You have a sweet boy and I love Curtis. He's always been so kind to my girls. However, they just reconnected their acquaintance at the wedding a little over 2 weeks ago. It's a little quick," Janet took another breath and Edward put his arm around her, "I'm just not sure about this. What seemed to be little trips together has blossomed into something more. To be honest, I worry about the age difference and the fact that Karen really hasn't been involved with anyone in a serious manner. As parents, I know you understand my concern."

"Yes," Abby managed to say. "He's a good son and knows to respect women. As a mother I would understand the concern with the age difference, especially with a young daughter." Abby looked at Owen, "We haven't really had any experience with this either. Keith and Florence were about the same age. Our daughter dated guys her own age as well." She touched her arm, "Janet, his dad and I can talk with Curtis and share our concerns." Owen nodded. Abby continued, "Curtis is waiting at the house. You'll see him in a few minutes."

Owen took a look at the car, "We were all worried about Florence seeing the house that Keith built for them. I know she never wanted to see it after he died."

Janet touched Owen's hand, "You're good people, and you have a nice family." She looked at Florence in the car, "We'll be there for her."

Abby inclined her head to Janet, "You should have everything you need. We made some casseroles and put them in the freezer. One is in the fridge if you all are hungry. Please call us if you need us. Florence can give you our number." The family got back in the car. Florence waved at the Daltons from her place in the back seat. They waved back and watched the car disappear around the bend. Owen put his arm around his wife who said, "I didn't realize they were dating, did you?"

He shook his head, "I guess by the way he acted in the coffee shop that day, we should have picked up on that. Abby, one thing at a time. He's a good kid, but I'll talk to him. I do understand a parent's concern about the age difference. If Leslie was dating someone ten years older, we would want to know his intentions. Maybe

Curtis can get her to talk about what happened so she can have some peace." Abby put her arms around her husband, and he kissed the top of her head. They held hands as they walked back into their home.

Love from Farm to Stable

Chapter 10

C urtis met them at the door. Florence walked with Karen and stopped at the threshold. She looked at the house and tears flowed down her face. He asked, "Florence, I worried about you seeing the house. Are you okay with this?" Florence touched the brass door knocker that Curtis's brother Keith had installed on the door. This was the house that Keith had built for them to move into once they were married.

"Yes, I'm okay. There was a lot of love that went into building this house. I never could bring myself to see the finished product. It was too painful at the time." He touched her shoulder. His gaze shifted to Karen. She hadn't looked at him. His heart was broken for her. He touched her arm and she pulled it back and hugged her sister. His eyes moistened as he stepped back to open the door. Janet and Edward walked in behind the girls.

Curtis managed to say, "I'll see to the luggage while you all get settled."

He was bringing in their suitcases when Riley pulled up. "Here, let me give you a hand," Riley helped him unload the car. As they checked once more to make sure everything had been brought into the house, Riley spoke to him, "Do you have a minute?" Curtis waited as Riley handed him a folder, "This is from Detective Myers. It's everything they have on the asshole."

"Thank you," said Curtis. Riley put his hand on his shoulder, and they walked into the house together. Florence was walking downstairs after getting Karen settled in one of the upstairs bedrooms. She walked to her husband and held on tight.

He searched his wife's face and kissed her, "How is she?"

"Hunt gave us something to help her sleep. She was drifting off when I left her."

Curtis spoke up, "Can I see her?"

Florence searched his eyes, which looked shattered. She touched his arm," Maybe in the morning. She's not doing too well responding to men right now." She gazed at Riley and then to the man who was like a brother to her, "Curtis, can I see you outside?" He gave her a resigned look and followed her. She sat on the swing as he leaned on the railing. She took a breath and said, "You're seeing my sister. How serious are you?"

He didn't quite know how to begin, so he just moved forward, "It started out as phone calls here and there. We'd go to lunch or take a drive. Then it became something more. Your sister and I had a long conversation about the age difference and decided it didn't matter to us. There was a discussion between us if it would be a concern for all of the parents and the siblings." He sat next to

Florence on the swing, "It's all so new to us. I never thought in a million years that we would be together. Sometimes life has a way of opening a window when one has already been closed."

Florence gazed at him and said, "You just ran into each other a couple of weeks ago at my wedding. She's not had too much experience with men if you understand what I'm saying. I feel like I can ask you to take care with that."

"I think that's something that needs to stay between your sister and me."

Florence explained, "I've taken care of her all our lives. I won't stop now just because she's an adult."

Curtis turned her way, "I love you, Florence, but I'm a little insulted you would ask. I was taught better than that. You know me. I'm not one of those men who's going to take advantage of your sister. I'm sure there will be plenty of people who would look at it that way with the age difference, but I never thought it would be you." He took a deep breath, "Yes, it's only been a couple of weeks, but sometimes the right person comes along. I know it's early yet, but she matters a great deal to me, Florence. Is that what you wanted to know?"

She touched his arm, "I love you too. I know you understand why I had to ask." He placed his hand on hers and nodded his head.

The door opened and Riley appeared on the porch, "Florence, Karen is asking for you." She patted Curtis's arm and got up from the swing. She walked to her husband and gently kissed him. He hugged her then she disappeared to check on her sister.

Riley joined him on the porch. He leaned against the railing while Curtis remained on the swing. He rested his elbows on his knees, looked up to Riley and asked, "Are you going to take a turn too?"

"Nah, I think my wife has probably made her point. These Smith women are awfully close. They've been through a lot and look out for each other. I'm not telling you anything you don't already know." Riley crossed his arms, "Karen is a sweet, caring person. As she's my sister in-law, I'd like her to have a good life with someone who is going to look out for her best interests."

Curtis sat up and stared at Riley, "Meaning?"

"I think that man is you. From my point of view, you've done nothing but be kind to her. Your family showed up at her job on her first day back, you've checked on her, talked with her and have been very supportive. I admit it's been a fast two weeks with you being together. I'm sure Florence got into some things with you that I'm not about to bring up. I'm sure I don't have to spell it out for you since you seem to respect her and want to take care of her."

"Just to clarify, "Curtis remarked, "You're not going to lecture me on the status of our relationship?"

Riley shook his head, "I don't have to talk about that with you. If you hurt her, I'll just kick your ass."

"Now, that I can understand," Curtis explained, "talking is so overrated."

They smiled at one another.

"Curtis," Florence stepped out onto the porch, "Karen's asking for you."

He took a deep breath and stopped at the door next to Florence, "I promise you I'll take care of her."

Florence touched his arm, "You're a good man, Curtis Dalton. Remember, I love you both and want what's best for each of you." He kissed her on the cheek and went to check on her sister.

She spotted Riley moving over to the swing. He looked up at his wife and patted the seat beside him. She stepped over to the swing and sat down next to him, "Come here often?" Riley asked.

"Yes," she responded, "but only when there's a sexy man available." He smiled. She looked at her watch, "He'll be here in a few minutes. You might want to make yourself scarce."

"You can be such a smartass."

"Yes, my husband tells me that often. But that's okay," she said, "because he still loves me." He leaned over and kissed her. She deepened the kiss.

As their lips parted, Riley said, "Yes, Mrs. Simmons, he loves you with all his heart." She put her head on his shoulder as they rocked back and forth on the swing.

Chapter 11

Curtis opened the door to Karen's room. She was sitting up in bed hugging her knees against her chest. He closed the door and settled his back against it as she turned towards him, "Hi Curtis."

He was so happy to see her, but he wanted her to set the tone, "Hi yourself."

She rested her head on top of her knees, "I wanted to tell you about my day."

"Okay, I'm listening," he looked at her gently.

"I worked at the shop today. I'm really glad to be back there. I'm content being in a routine."

"I'm glad, Karen."

"Would you like to sit down?"

He looked around the room and the only place to sit was the bed, "I'm fine here. Thank you."

"Okay," Karen paused, "I really liked being with you last night. When you came by the shop this morning, it was such a surprise. I didn't expect to see you so soon and it meant a lot to me because you make me happy."

"I'm happy when I'm with you too." She hugged her knees and smiled at him, then her smile dimmed as she continued to talk.

"After you left the shop, I was moving inventory around inside when the man who assaulted me drove by. I'll never forget the look on his face. It was the look of privilege, of having whatever he wanted," her voice broke. He stood up straight as Karen continued, "He winked at me." Tears began to trickle down her face, "Then he was gone, like it never happened." She began to cry softly. She cleared her throat and he moved further into the room. "He's going to try again. I'm so afraid he's going to find me and when he does, I'm so scared he's going to…that he's going to…" She began to sob.

He couldn't take it anymore. He couldn't stand by and watch her fall apart. He slowly sat on the bed facing her and settled her in his arms. He ran his hand gently down her hair, "I'm not going to let that happen. I'm going to do everything in my power to stop him, so that you can feel safe again. My family will take care of you. I will take care of you."

Karen wiped her eyes and said, "You and I will take care of each other."

He held her tighter, "Yes, we will." Still holding her, Curtis reached over on the bed stand and picked up the box of tissues. He began to dry her eyes.

She took his hand and brushed her cheek with it, "Would you kiss me?"

"With what you've been through today, I don't know if that's such a good idea." She placed her hands on his cheeks, leaned forward, and touched her lips to his. She then sat back. He lost himself in those pretty green eyes. He stood up and took her with him. He held her and she wrapped her arms around him.

"Curtis?"

"Hmm?"

"You make me feel so safe." She moved back slightly and kissed him on the cheek, "You make me feel needed." She kissed his other cheek, "You make me feel wanted." Karen locked eyes with him as they moved towards each other. His lips touched hers then roamed over her face as he kissed her forehead, her eyes, her cheeks and then her mouth. Karen rested her head on his shoulder, and he held her, "I have something to ask you, Curtis."

"Yes?" he said.

She spied the books on the shelf, "Will you read to me until I fall asleep?"

"On one condition," he looked at her with an amused expression, "I'm over 30 and can't believe I'm about to say this, but we have to leave the door open. There are parents in the house and it's just the right thing to do."

She laughed and said, "I think you're right. It's like an unwritten rule, isn't it?"

"One more thing before we open the door," he held her face in his hands, "I need you too." He kissed her softly on the mouth and opened the door. Curtis spied a chair in the hallway and brought it into the room. She had situated herself under the covers resting her head on her pillow. "Okay, which book?" he asked.

"Pride and Prejudice." she answered.

"Seriously, you want me to read a chick book?"

"It's Jane Austen. It's a classic. You might even like it. Have you ever read it?" He gave her a disbelieving look. "It's all about Elizabeth Bennet and Mr. Darcy, who have to get over their thoughts and preconceived notions in order to be together. It's very romantic." He didn't say anything, "Well, what do you read?" she asked.

"The Farmer's Almanac, Corn Growers Association newsletter, Alabama Farmers Federation Magazine, the sports section when Auburn plays football..."

"Curtis, we've got to get you out more." He sighed and picked up the book. He looked at her one more time. She had a twinkle in her eye.

"You do know you're beautiful, don't you?"

"I'll take your word for it." she said.

Curtis opened the book, "Chapter 1." He began to read. By the time he started Chapter 3, he felt a stillness in the room and heard her steady breathing. She had fallen asleep. He got up and settled the covers over her. He brushed his lips on her forehead, "Sleep well," he whispered. He placed the book on the table by the bed and turned out the lamp. He silently made his way out of the room. Janet and Florence had been sitting outside the room listening to him read to Karen, "If you ever tell anyone I read that book out loud, I'll deny it to my everlasting day."

Florence responded, "We all love that book. We couldn't resist a chance to listen to it read aloud."

Janet nodded her head and smiled, "Yes, we love that book."

Florence had a gleam in her eye, "Curtis, you really should think about reading books for those books on tape deals. You have a very seductive voice. Women would be falling all over themselves trying to buy your tapes. It could be a second career for you." Florence tried to hold it together, but she couldn't contain her laughter. Her eyes watered. Janet smiled.

"You're a real piece of work, you know that Florence?" He looked at Janet, "Goodnight, Mrs. Smith." Curtis hastened down the stairs and let himself out.

Love from Farm to Stable

Chapter 12

After Thanksgiving, everyone on the farm settled into a routine. Curtis made his daily rounds, traveled locally on farm business and would sometimes join Karen's family for lunch or dinner. Janet went to work while Edward stayed close. Abby and Owen would join the family at times for dinner or the family would come to the Big House. Janet was complimentary of Abby's blueberry cobbler. Abby loved Janet's chicken tetrazzini. When the dinner dishes were cleared and families had settled in their houses for the night, Curtis would read to Karen. She would settle in her bed and listen to the story of Elizabeth Bennet and Mr. Darcy as they argued with each other and would come to understand one another on their way to being together.

Sometimes Florence and Janet would come up to listen for a while. Chairs had been moved in for comfort. Curtis's sister, Leslie, had a huge rocker installed in the room. She thought maybe rocking would soothe Karen if there were nights she couldn't sleep. He had only been told of a couple of nights that had been difficult for her.

Otherwise, she seemed to relax when he would read to her. On one night, Curtis had been reading a chapter and was so entranced by the story, he didn't realize Karen had fallen asleep. He got up to stretch. Janet and Florence had left the room earlier and everyone in the house was asleep. He was placing the book on the bedside table when she began to toss and turn. As he went to place a hand on her arm to help calm her, she gasped and sat straight up in bed. "Hey, I'm here." She wildly stared at him, "It's me." He sat down on the edge of the bed.

"Curtis?" Karen moved into his arms and he held her.

"Want to talk about it?"

She shook her head, "I know it's late, but would you stay with me a little longer, at least until I go back to sleep?" He looked at the open door and had an idea. He saw a small quilt folded on the end of the bed and wrapped it around her.

He gazed at Karen as he picked her up in his arms, "Hold onto me." She put her arms around his neck. He carried her to the rocker and held her on his lap. She laid her head on his shoulder and cuddled with him. He put his arms around her and began to rock. She lifted her head and touched her mouth to his. She moved her head back to his shoulder and held him. The steady movement of the rocker and the comfort of being held by each other lulled them both to sleep.

During the wee hours of the morning, Janet went to check on her daughter. She smiled at the scene that greeted her. Curtis held Karen in the rocker as they both slept. Janet hadn't been sure at first about the age difference, but now it didn't seem to matter. She and her daughter would have a talk. She tiptoed into the room, took the cover off the bed and gently covered them both. She turned the lamp off and closed the door.

A rooster could be heard crowing in the early morning hours and Curtis opened his eyes. He had fallen asleep holding Karen. He noticed someone had closed the door. It was probably her mom checking on her during the night. He felt her stir. Her eyes opened and met his. She touched his face and leaned in for a kiss. He responded in kind and the kiss deepened. They slowly broke apart, "Good morning, Curtis."

He couldn't help but smile at her, "Good morning, Karen."

"What's on your agenda for today?" she asked.

He looked at his watch. "Well, it's 5AM. We can stay just like this for another 15 minutes or I can go home now." Karen answered Curtis by laying her head on his chest. "Okay, 15 minutes it is," he responded. He kissed the top of her head and sat quietly with her. After their time was up, he kissed her once more as she got back into bed and fell asleep. Curtis walked down the steps holding his jacket and made his way to the door. As his hand landed on the doorknob, he was interrupted by Edward joining him in the room.

"Good morning, Curtis."

Curtis turned and said, "Edward."

Edward folded his arms, "Any reason you're coming downstairs from the vicinity of Karen's room at 5:30 in the morning looking sleep deprived? You know in my father's day this would be cause for a display of a shotgun."

"She had a nightmare during the night while I was still here. She was unsettled and asked me to stay for a while until she could fall back to sleep." He eyed Edward, "Being the gentleman that my father and mother raised, I sat in the rocking chair with her all night. We both fell asleep. Her mother must have checked on us during the night, because when I woke up this morning the door was closed, and someone had put a blanket over us. When we both woke up this morning, being the loving and kind person Karen is, she kissed me. Since I was holding a beautiful woman who matters very much to me, I kissed her back. That covers our night together." Curtis faced Edward and waited.

"Well, Son. I hope you have a good day. But just remember, I do have a shotgun that I could show you at any time if I feel the need. You'd agree with me on that right?"

"If I had a daughter and I saw a man coming out of her room, it's what I would do. Have a good day, sir." Curtis walked out of the house and closed the door. He stopped on the porch, ran his hand through his hair and exhaled, "I'm getting too old for this." He took a deep breath, made his way to his truck and headed home.

When Karen woke up that morning, she decided a routine would be best. Her boss had checked on her. Maybe there was a way to return to work. Her boss thought about closing the dining room for a while and installing a drive by window. It was a thought in progress. In the meantime, she needed something physical to do. She got Abby's phone number from her mom and dialed. Thirty minutes later, she was on her way to the stables.

Later that day, Curtis was making his rounds on the farm when his phone rang, "Hey, Dad. What's up? You need me to go to the stables? Any particular reason why? You need me to do a pickup there?" He shook his head as this wasn't on the schedule today, "Okay. I'll head there now." Curtis drove the winding road to the stables. He stopped the truck and looked around for equipment or products for storage. When he didn't see anything, he went inside the stables.

He was dumbfounded. Outfitted in gloves and rubber boots, Karen held a shovel and was cleaning out stalls. She was dirty from her head to her feet. He noticed another person helping her. His mom handed her a pitchfork. There were several wheelbarrows in use. They had found an old radio, which currently was playing 70's music...very loud 70's music. His gaze moved to the old wooden table in the corner of the room, which held an empty gallon jug and 2 red solo cups.

He looked at the two women again. His mom was blowing hair out of her eyes disheveled by cleaning out stalls. Her cheek was dirty, and her boots were caked with mud. It had been years since he'd seen her mucking out stalls. He watched his mom turn up the radio. She yelled to Karen, "It's the Hustle. Come on!" She started dancing and Karen joined her. Curtis heard a truck. He turned to see his dad walk into the stables.

He stood next to Curtis and grinned. "Um Dad, what do we do here?"

Owen laughed and said, "Well, I'm going to take your mom home. I'll let you figure out the rest." Owen walked towards his wife. She flung her arms out to hug him and he steered her at arm's length outside. He grabbed a blanket from his truck bed, laid it on the front seat and got his wife into the truck. He rolled the window down, "You might want to grab an empty feed bucket in case she gets sick." His dad looked towards the empty jug. Owen smiled," You got it Son?"

Curtis looked at Karen dancing around, "Yeah, Dad, piece of cake." His dad winked at him and drove Curtis's mother home. He took a deep breath and walked towards Karen.

She spotted him and ran towards him for a hug. He stopped her at arms' length. Up closer it was much worse than he thought. She was covered in mud everywhere. "Did you shovel today or just roll in the mud?" Whew, he thought. That was a lot more than just mud. He went to one of the cabinets to get a towel they kept stocked.

Curtis took her hand and said, "Come with me." They stepped out of the back door of the stables and he picked up the hose. Karen took a deep breath and was finally able to focus on him. He asked her to stand still, and he turned on the hose.

"Why are you turning on that hose?"

"This is going to be cold at first, but trust me, it's the only way to get that mud off."

"Curtis Dalton, don't you dare."

"Close your eyes." He stepped closer to her and turned the hose on her hair, her shoulders, her midsection, her legs then her feet, until the mud was running down in rivulets towards the ground.

She was shivering, "Curtis, that's cold! Just wait until I tell your mother!"

"What do you think my dad is doing right now? This is how we all got cleaned up when we had to muck out stalls growing up. Alright now, let's towel you off." Curtis rubbed her hair and began drying her off. He could feel the perspiration break out on his forehead as he touched her. This was not going to be easy. She was shivering. He took her hand to lead her back through the stables, grabbing a dry towel and a blanket. He helped Karen wrap the towel around her while walking to the truck. After he made her comfortable, he trotted around to his side. Driving to his house, he glanced at her face, which was losing color. He increased his speed and landed at his house in no time. He got her through the door and guided her to the small bathroom next to the laundry room. She made it just in time as she leaned over the toilet. He held a washcloth under the cool water from the sink. He waited until she was finished and pressed the cool washcloth on her forehead. She held it there, took a deep cleansing breath and sat against the back wall of the bathroom.

She closed her eyes and said, "Curtis Dalton, you have some explaining to do."

He raised an eyebrow and squatted down until they were eye to eye, "I have some explaining to do? When I got to the stables, my sainted mother and you were three sheets to the wind judging from the empty gallon jug, solo cups and the dancing going on."

"Dancing? Who was dancing?"

Now that things had calmed down, Curtis grinned, "You and my mother were dancing to 70's oldies music."

"Curtis, you have lost your mind." She pressed the washcloth to her head, "Your mother made mimosas and we were cleaning out the stalls. I wanted to listen to music. She found this old radio." She looked up at him, "Oh, it's all coming back now." She held the cloth on her forehead and closed her eyes.

"Welcome back. How about we get you in a hot shower and you can lie down for a while?"

She opened one eye and noticed this was a guest bathroom without a shower or tub. "I don't think I can move." She looked so pitiful sitting there he thought.

"Take my hand." She put her hand in his and he pulled her up. She swayed. He picked her up and carried her to the shower down the hall. He leaned in and turned on the water, "Okay, hop in." She looked at him and he said, "Sorry, bad choice of words. Okay, in you go. You'll see a washcloth and a towel on the back wall." Karen carefully got in the shower and he closed the curtain, "There's a laundry basket on the floor here. You can drop your clothes in it." Curtis waited. He saw Karen's hand come through the curtain. She dropped her jeans and her shirt in the basket. Then came the bra. He broke out in a sweat. Her underwear landed on top of the bra. He leaned against the bathroom counter while his thoughts centered on her on the other side of the shower curtain.

He heard the water turn off, "Okay, Curtis." He saw her hand come through the curtain again. The towel and washcloth hit the basket. He was in trouble here. He grabbed the robe he kept on the hook attached to the door and handed it to her through the curtain. She pulled the curtain back. Dressed in the robe, she held her hand out to him. He tried not to think about what was underneath that robe as he took her hand to help her out of the shower. He watched her to make sure she was steady on her feet, "Okay?" Curtis asked.

"Um, if there are two of you, I'm okay." Then she proceeded to pass out. He caught her before she hit the floor.

Karen's eyes flew open. She sat up in a strange bed. She looked around and saw Abby and her mom sitting in chairs near her bed. Curtis walked into the room holding a cup of coffee and handed it to Janet. He saw a movement out of the corner of his eye and saw that she was awake, "Hi there."

"Hi, yourself, Curtis. What happened?"

"You don't remember?" he asked incredulously.

117

"I remember taking your hand to get out of the shower."

Both mothers swiveled their heads towards him. Curtis kept his gaze fixed on Karen but held a hand up to them, "Not what you're thinking." Janet glanced at her daughter.

"I had the robe on you had given me," She looked down at a big t-shirt and leggings covering her. She looked at him. He pointed to Janet and Karen continued, "I don't remember anything after that."

Curtis looked at his mom and said to Karen, "You passed out."

Abby spoke up, "Karen, I want to apologize. I think I'm at fault for this. Maybe we should have just stuck with water. I'll know better next time." Curtis stared at his mother. "Curtis Dalton, I've apologized. You'll need to watch that tone of voice with me. I'm still your mother."

"Mom, I didn't even say anything."

"Oh, you don't have to. Your eyes speak volumes," She put her hand to her head. Curtis sighed and walked out of the room.

"Is everything okay with Curtis?" asked Karen.

"He's annoyed with me, because I provided the mimosas."

"That's not the only reason I passed out, Mrs. Dalton," said Karen. He returned with a glass of water and Tylenol and handed them to his mother.

Karen continued talking, "I didn't eat anything today. I just didn't think. The combination of the drinks and nothing on my stomach probably didn't help. Sorry."

Her mom spoke up, "You think you can make it home with me?"

"Yes, ma'am," Karen tried to stand up and immediately had to sit back on the bed. Curtis walked forward and took her hand. She said, "Oh, my head is spinning."

Janet walked around him to put her hand on her daughter's forehead, "Oh, Honey, you're burning up."

Abby glanced at her son, "Do you have any of my homemade soup left in your freezer?" He nodded and walked out of the room with his mom to the kitchen.

Janet followed them, "Do you have any Advil?" Curtis took a bottle out of his cabinet. He poured a glass of water and gave both to Karen's mom. "Thank you," she walked back to the bedroom.

Curtis got the soup out of the freezer. His mom put the soup in a large pot. He leaned against the counter and watched her slice her homemade bread he kept in his kitchen, "I'm sorry mom."

"I'm sorry too," she said as she kept slicing the bread.

"I didn't mean to sass you. Karen has become important to me and I don't want anything to happen to her."

A tear fell down his mom's cheek. She turned to face him, "You're all grown up. I just can't believe how fast time flies." He hugged his mom. She leaned back and brushed a hand over his hair. With tears in her eyes, she asked, "How's my handsome son?"

"He's glad he has a mom like you. I love you, Mom."

"Oh, Curtis, you and Keith always knew what to say to make me cry." He hugged his mom and smiled up at heaven.

Chapter 13

Curtis walked around his house turning off the lights, making sure doors were locked and turning on the alarm system. After everyone had their fill of homemade soup and bread, Janet and Abby had a discussion with him. With the dizziness and fever, they thought it best not to move Karen. Hunt even made an appearance after Florence told him her sister was sick. He thought she had just picked up a virus and would be well in a couple of days. He left some medicine for her. After Curtis fixed him a bowl of homemade soup and a slice of fresh bread, he was on his way home. Curtis sauntered to his guest bedroom. He leaned against the doorframe and crossed his arms. He watched Karen in the shadows from the moonlight coming through the window. Walking to the side of the bed where she was sleeping, he leaned down and brushed her hair out of her face. He kissed her forehead. She was still warm to the touch. He looked on the bedside table and saw the cold compress. He gently placed it on her forehead. Even in sickness, she was beautiful. She turned over to the side where he was standing. Karen opened her eyes, "Hi Curtis."

He sat on the edge of the bed, "Hi yourself. How are you feeling?"

"Not great. I'm hot."

"Hang on, be right back." Curtis walked to his freezer and filled a small plastic bag with ice. He refilled her water cup and returned to the room, "Let's try this. Can you sit up for me?"

Karen sat up slowly. He sat on the bed and placed the ice bag on the back of her neck. "Oh, that's cold!"

"Give it a few minutes."

She gazed at his warm brown eyes, "Thank you, Curtis, for taking care of me."

He looked at her pretty green eyes, "You're welcome. I'm glad you're staying here. It's nice to be alone with you."

"Yes, it is, even if I'm sick and can't hold you or kiss you."

Curtis had a twinkle in his eye, "Oh, we'll make up for that when you're better." He leaned over to kiss her on the head, and she sneezed.

"I'm sorry, Curtis," she said. He handed her the box of tissues and grabbed a small trash can for her to throw her tissues away.

"It's okay. How about I let you get some sleep?" He helped her get settled. She laid her head on her pillow and began to drift off to sleep.

"Sweet dreams," he whispered.

"You too, Curtis." Then she slept.

A bloodcurdling scream woke Curtis and had him flying out of his bed into Karen's room. As he landed in the doorway, he could see Karen sitting up and shaking. She was hugging her knees to her chest and tears were rolling down her face, "Curtis! Curtis!" she held out her arms to him. He scooped her up and leaned back against the headboard.

He put his cheek next to hers, "Hey, I'm right here. I'm not going to let anything happen to you."

"Curtis, please don't leave me alone."

As he held her, he heard his cell phone ring, "Hey, it might be an emergency. I promise you I'll be right back. Okay?" She nodded, shaking, as she pulled her knees to her chest. As he reached for the phone on his bedroom dresser, he saw the number on the screen, "Leslie? You heard screaming? Yes, she stayed over. Mom told you she was sick?" Sometimes, Curtis forgot that his sister lived on land that was practically outside his back door. Curtis walked back to Karen's room and his eyes met hers, "She had a bad nightmare. You don't have to come over, but I appreciate the offer. I'm going to sit up with her for a while. Yes, I'll tag you in the morning. Thanks Sis." He laid his phone on the dresser. Karen was shivering. He covered her up, then got in on the other side of the bed. She reached for him and he held her, "Do you want to tell me about it?"

She clung to him tighter, "The man broke in. You tried to stop him, and he killed you." She was sobbing,

"Curtis, then he…. then he…. after it was over, he pointed a gun at my face. Then I woke up."

He cleared his throat and held her tight, "Karen, I'm going to help you. He's not going to have a chance to get anywhere near you. He has more than one person on this farm to go through than just me. We know how to protect ourselves and to protect you. I know who the bastard is now, so we have a name to put with the face." He kissed the top of her head and she snuggled closer to him, "Here, lie down now." He made sure she had a comfortable pillow and had pulled the covers over her once again.

As he moved off the bed, Karen held his arm. With desperation showing in her eyes, she begged, "Please don't leave me. Please."

He stared at her and made a decision, "Okay, let's try this. Turn over so I can hold you." He laid on top of the covers and pulled her in, so they were nestled like two spoons. He put his arms around her, and she crossed her hands over his arms.

She breathed easier and said, "Thank you, Curtis."

He kissed her on the head, "Anytime."

The shadows during the night disappeared with the rising of the sun. Curtis raised his head to check on Karen. She was in a deep sleep still nestled in his arms. He laid his head back on his pillow and savored this time with her holding her close. His eyes closed and he fell back to sleep. He woke up an hour later. Karen had turned over and was staring at him.

"Hi Curtis," her eyes lit up in a smile.

"Hi yourself," he brushed her hair out of her eyes, "How are you feeling?"

She covered her mouth as she yawned, "I think I'm better. I'm just extremely tired."

"There's no reason why you can't sleep a little while longer right here, but I will have to get up soon. I have a few errands to run today."

Karen smiled, "Can you stay right here with me a little while longer?"

He gazed into her eyes as his heart began to race, "Um, I'm not so sure that's such a good idea." His finger caressed her cheek.

"Curtis, I really like holding you. I'd like to kiss you."

Curtis felt beads of perspiration breaking out on his forehead. He thought he could settle for a kiss. His eyes met hers, "One kiss, Karen Smith, then I'm getting out of this bed." She scooted closer to him and touched her mouth to his. His hand moved to stroke her hair and his hand then held her cheek as the kiss deepened. Curtis moved closer to her. His mouth roamed to her forehead. He took a breath and gazed into her eyes, "Karen." His mouth touched hers once more and he was lost. She took a breath herself after their kiss.

She looked at him imploringly, "There's something I need to tell you."

He picked up her hand and kissed it. She gazed into his warm brown eyes, which were filled with desire. "Curtis, I...." The cell phone on the dresser began to ring.

"We could ignore it," he kissed her forehead then his mouth moved down her cheek. The phone stopped ringing, then started again. They looked at each other. He kissed her gently on the mouth, "Be right back."

"Yeah, hey Dad," Curtis glanced over at her, "Yes, I think she's feeling better. I'm making breakfast soon. Oh, you'll be over in thirty minutes with muffins from mom. Yes, Dad. See you then." he put his phone on the dresser and looked at her, "Do you know how beautiful you are?" He went to sit on the side of the bed and kissed her softly on the lips, "I'd like to take up where we left off, but I guess it will have to keep for now." She had a worried look on her face. He asked her, "You wanted to tell me something?" He put his hand on her forehead. She was cool to the touch.

She moved forward and kissed him, "We'll talk later, okay? Your dad will be here soon."

"You sure? You're worried about something. I can see it all over your face. You can talk to me about anything, you do know that?"

Karen looked at Curtis. He was a wonderful man. He was kind and so good to her. She trusted him to be gentle and understanding with her when she finally got out what she had to say to him. Now was not the time since they were about to have company. "Yes," she put a hand on his cheek. He kissed her hand. "I think I'll go take a shower," she said as she spied her clothes folded on the chair by the door, "Thank you for washing my clothes."

"I do what I can," He smiled as he looked down at her. He gave her his arm to help her up, "No dizziness?"

"Not so far," she kissed him and hugged him. She let him go and noticed his pajamas. "Really? The ball cap wasn't enough?" He looked down at his Auburn t-shirt and matching bottoms.

He grinned, "Christmas present from Keith."

She touched his face and kissed his mouth, "Tell him I forgive him."

He kissed her back and hugged her, "Go take your shower. Dad will be here with bells on."

Twenty minutes later, Karen came out to see Owen and Curtis setting the table, "Hi Hon. How are you?" His dad stepped up to Karen and touched her forehead, "Cool as a cucumber."

"Hi Mr. Owen," She grinned as she couldn't help but like Curtis's dad.

"How about you call me Owen, so you don't make me feel like I've got one foot in the grave."

"Yes, sir," She caught his look, "Owen."

"There ya' go," He pulled a chair out for her, "Here, have a seat, Hon. Abby made a variety of muffins." He passed her the basket.

Curtis came to stand beside her chair and touched her shoulder. He put out her medicine and a glass of water, "Coffee or juice?"

"Water will be fine for now. Thank you."

He winked at her, "You bet." Karen ate part of a muffin and drank her water. They all talked a little about the news and Christmas in a few weeks.

Owen remarked, "We were thinking about having something at the house. How does that sound, you two? Maybe Christmas lunch or dinner?"

Curtis gazed at Karen and smiled. She put her hand on his and said it sounded good to her. She could get with her mom and Florence about bringing something to their house. Owen noticed the looks between the two of them. He sighed quietly and remembered when Abby and he fell in love. It was time to head on back to the house.

Owen winked at her, "Anything you want to bring to the house that day would be fine Hon."

Curtis talked about his errands he needed to run after dropping Karen off at the house. He glanced at her, "That is, unless you'd like to go with me? Unless you aren't feeling well or have schoolwork to finish?"

Her eyes warmed when she looked at Curtis, "I'd like that. I'm good with school right now." Owen noticed those pretty green eyes sparkle when she looked at his son. Of course, Curtis had eyes only for her. He would have to tell Abby it looked like they would be planning a wedding in the future.

"Okay, Son. Think I can see you outside for a minute?"

"Sure Dad. Tell Mom thanks for the muffins."

"Sure will," Owen looked at Karen. He came around to her chair and put his hand on her forehead,

"Still cool as a cucumber. Just don't let my son run you ragged today. Get some rest."

"Yes, sir." He gave her that look. "Owen."

"There you go. Take care Hon." Curtis smiled at Karen and followed his dad to the porch and closed the door. Owen put his hand on Curtis's shoulder, "I wanted to tell you that Abby felt terrible about yesterday at the stables. She worried all afternoon. She said you weren't very happy with her."

"Dad, we're good now." His dad looked at Curtis, "I apologized to her."

"Yes, we raised good children who respect their parents. She's the only mom you'll ever have. Remember to be good to her. She loves her children very much." His dad hugged him and said, "So do I."

"I know Dad," he hugged his father, "Dad, before you go, I wanted to tell you something." Owen waited. "I want to come over in the morning and talk to you and mom. I received the folder of information about the asshole that assaulted Karen. I want to come up with a plan. She had a horrible nightmare last night. I'd like to take care of this situation once and for all." His eyes moistened, "She shouldn't have to live like this, Dad."

Owen spoke up, "Just a thought Son, but do you think she'll let you teach her how to shoot a gun, for protection? I've been meaning to tell Edward about our shooting range. I believe he's already established in his, but he might like going somewhere closer. He probably wouldn't mind helping. What do you think?"

"I'm not sure Dad. She does have some steel underneath that gentleness. I'll talk with her about it."

Owen placed his hand on Curtis's shoulder, "Just let me know, Son. We all like her and we want the best for her, okay?" Curtis nodded. His dad climbed into his truck, pulled on his ball cap and sunglasses, "We'll see you in the morning."

Curtis put his hands in his pockets while he watched his dad drive away. He would feel better if Karen could defend herself. He would talk with her. She had something else on her mind, and he hoped she would feel more comfortable talking with him. He thought it had to do with this morning. If his dad hadn't called, he wasn't sure what would have happened. He wanted her, but if she wasn't ready, he would wait for her. He didn't want to take advantage of her vulnerability. Not many men would do that, as he thought about the bastard who hurt her. Curtis would see his parents tomorrow and then he would take the next step.

Clarence Higgins, III sat at a table in a local hamburger joint and tried not to show his disgust for his surroundings. He was a 5-star man in a 1-star restaurant, if that's what you wanted to call it. Clarence was waiting for his companion, who was finally back from her trip. He gave a smile to the young, leggy blonde who brought him a Vodka. His smile didn't reach his eyes, but she didn't notice. She smiled back at him, probably for the tip, he thought. She walked away and he saw the back of her legs. They would have been pretty except for the tattoos. He shook his head. Why mess up a good pair of legs with that cheap art? He watched his guest walk through the door. Talk about a good pair of legs and she had no tattoos from what he remembered. He smirked. She put her bag on the chair next to her and sat across from him. Clarence watched her swing her long dark brunette hair over her shoulder. He remembered when that hair caressed his bare chest. He was getting aroused, but he had to remember he was here on business.

"So, Clarence, what is all this about?" Marlena Taylor asked.

Clarence leaned forward and said, "In due time, Marlena. For old times' sake, I need your help with something."

Marlena sat up straight in her chair. If her dad had not gotten sick that time, she never would have started up with Clarence. They met each other at the country club. Her mom came from old money and those relatives still had a membership. When her dad was diagnosed with leukemia the relatives couldn't take the time to help nor was her dad going to ask them for the money. He was a proud man. Her dad thought Marlena had talked to the insurance company and that's how he was able to keep up with treatments, along with selling off land from the farm. That's where Clarence had come into the picture. He came across with the money in exchange for several weeks in his bed. She couldn't summon up the courage to care. Any goodness in her life stopped the day she left Curtis Dalton. She had wanted more at the time. His mom got sick, and she wanted the attention on her. She had been selfish and stupid. She had lost a good man.

Marlena still kept her ear to the ground and heard he had been dating someone several years younger than him. The girl was probably good to him. That's the only way Curtis would be close to someone. He thought at one time, she had good in her. But he finally saw the truth. Not like the man sitting across from her. The man across from her cared only about himself. He was a nasty piece of work. After she stopped sleeping with him, she heard stories about him around town tainted with assaults and even accusations of rape from several women. No one could ever prove anything because she learned his daddy had taken care of everything.

She sipped her water the waitress had placed on the table and asked, "Why should I help you? Our negotiations have been over for quite some time."

He casually placed his hand on hers and began to squeeze it. From any observer looking at their table, it would look like two people holding hands. But Clarence subtly dug his nails into her lower wrist without anyone being the wiser, "I'm sure you don't want me to call your father to let him know how naughty his daughter has been and the reason why, now do you?"

She winced with the pain of his fingernails digging into her skin as horror showed in her eyes. She loved her father, but he'd never understand what she had done to save him. She hissed out a breath as he let her hand go and asked, "What do I have to do?"

"Well, Marlena, I'd thought you'd never ask." He leaned forward and began to tell her the plan.

Love from Farm to Stable

Chapter 14

Curtis took a glimpse over at Karen as he drove them around town running errands. He reached over and put his hand on hers. She squeezed his hand and had a happy expression on her face. She hadn't mentioned what had her worried this morning. He would give her time and hoped she would talk to him soon. He put his hand back on the steering wheel and pulled up at the Feed and Seed. He stood in line to pick up their order for the farm, while she browsed in the garden section.

Curtis was waiting at the checkout when he noticed a young man wearing a work apron ask Karen if she needed any help. He was pointing to several plants. She smiled as they talked for a few minutes. He nodded his head and moved on. Curtis watched him turn back and smile at Karen. She was oblivious to the man's smile. She walked further down the aisle with several displays of metal art. A man who looked to be a little older than Curtis stopped to talk with her. He watched Karen's mouth curve as the man showed her a tall metal turtle with a flowerpot attached to his stomach. She then laughed at something he said. The man waved and walked down the next aisle.

Curtis moved up in line at the counter. Karen walked around a fountain display until she stopped to look at the variety of flags hanging on the wall. An elderly gentleman walking with a cane stepped up to stand by her. He tipped his hat at Karen which displayed a branch of the military. She nodded her head. The man looked for a few minutes at each flag. He turned to Karen and spoke to her. She stepped forward and picked out a flag with a picture of a red cardinal perched on a bird bath. A smile bloomed on the old soldier's face. He leaned closer to her and said something. She nodded and raised her hand. The man landed a kiss on the back of her hand. He winked at her and slowly made his way to the counter.

Curtis saw her gaze at the man and then she took a few steps to catch up with him. The man looked at her quizzically. Karen spoke to him. He inclined his head and she hugged him. When she released him, he said something to her. She looked up and pointed towards Curtis. The man took off his hat and nodded. Curtis nodded back at the older gentleman, who turned back to the counter. Karen traveled back down the aisle until she reached the man she was falling in love with. He finished at the counter, walked out with her and watched as his order was loaded into the back of his truck.

"I don't know if I can bring you back here." Karen looked at him with a question in her eyes. "You've charmed every man in this place. So, the next time we have to pick up an order here, I'd have to stand in line just to talk to you," his eyes crinkled, and he then grinned from ear to ear. He opened her door for her. She put a hand on his cheek and softly kissed his lips. He pulled her to him and hugged her. He closed his eyes and thanked God he had found her. When he released her, he brushed her hair back from her eyes and waited while she got in the truck. He closed her door and trotted around to his side of the truck. Curtis stopped at the door and felt as if someone was watching him. His gaze settled on the elderly man with the military hat whose car was parked close to his truck. The man had a tear falling from his eye. Curtis walked over to him. The man clasped his hand. Karen had turned her head to see where Curtis had gone and saw him talking with the elderly gentleman. She watched him nod as he opened the door for the man. The man started his car and drove off.

Curtis climbed into the truck and looked at Karen. His eyes had moistened as he pulled her close to him. She hugged him back. "He told me you helped him pick out a flag to honor his wife who had passed on. He said she loved birds. You suggested a red cardinal because that means when someone dies, they take the shape of a cardinal. He said he had one visiting recently in his backyard. He was happy when you told him she had come for a visit." Karen held on to him and heard him say, "The man's name is Gary Rogers and he's 85 years old. He told me I better hang on to you, because there aren't many kind and loving people left in the world. We reminded him of how he and his wife would hug and kiss. He told me I was a lucky man." He leaned back and wiped his eyes, "I agreed with him." His gaze centered on her, "Thank you for being with me."

Tears ran down Karen's face, "Curtis, we're both lucky."

He leaned across and kissed her, then sat back in his seat, "Ready?"

She touched his arm, "Yes, I'm ready." He winked at her and they drove to their next destination. Once they completed their errands, he pulled up to a restaurant attached to a marina.

Turning to Karen, he asked if she was hungry. She replied, "I'm starving."

"Let's get something to eat so you can take your medicine." He opened her door for her, and they walked up the steps to the restaurant. Since the weather was sunny and mild, they decided to sit outside for lunch.

Karen gazed at all the sailboats and charter boats, "They're all pretty." He asked her if she'd ever been sailing. "I went one time with a few friends from college. One of their families had a bay house and they had a sailboat they called a sloop. I remember it was fun until I watched an alligator pop up by the boat. That was my last time on a sailboat." The waiter stopped by their table to deliver glasses of water. They declined drinks, "How about you? Ever been on a sailboat?"

A smile crossed his face, "Keith, Leslie and I decided to rent a sailboat when Keith graduated from high school. Our parents had rented a bay house and there was a boat place down from the house. None of us really knew what we were doing. We started drifting further from the house and none of us could figure out how to maneuver a sailboat with no wind. We were all arguing, when the marine police pulled up to our boat and told us if we started the motor attached to the back, we'd get home a lot faster." Curtis smiled at the memory, "We never thought to look on the back of the boat."

Karen propped her chin on her hand and her mouth turned up, "Sounds like you three were close. It's nice to have a sibling."

"Yes, it is." He glanced at the water and a sadness touched his eyes. She put her hand on his arm, and he patted her hand, "Karen, what did you want to tell me this morning? I know you're worried about something." The waiter interrupted by asking if they had decided about lunch. Curtis took a breath and asked what she wanted to order.

Once they gave their orders, she looked at him, "You want me to talk about this now?" She looked around. They were far away from the few tables filled with people.

"We're alone with no other interruptions, and I'd like you to be able to relax. Maybe once you talk about it, you won't worry."

She stared at him," I'll still worry about how you'll take this news." He noticed she was nervous, so he waited.

"I've never been with another man. I'm a little uncomfortable when we get to a certain point when we...."

when we...." Karen had a hard time finishing her sentence.

Curtis held out his hand, "You're talking about this morning when we were in bed together?"

She put her hand in his and nodded her head, "I felt so close to you this morning. I enjoyed kissing you. Then I felt that our kissing was turning into something more. I'm not ready to go any further. That's why I wanted to talk to you." She blew out a breath.

"I won't pretend with you. I do want you, very much. I like holding you and touching you too," he cleared his throat, "It's a natural progression to what the kissing and touching may lead to when you and I are together."

"Curtis, I know that. I'm a smart person. I just haven't had this type of experience with a man."

"Karen, this isn't a deal breaker. I'm happy to wait for you because I want to be with you. There's no one else. I don't want anyone else. But I need you to trust me enough to be honest with me, to tell me what you like and don't like."

Relief showed on her face, "I can do that."

Curtis continued, "When the time is right, we'll know." He picked up her hand and kissed it. Their food arrived and they had an enjoyable lunch. She was able to relax now that she had talked to him. After lunch, he asked if she'd like to take a walk on the pier that led to the marina. They walked hand in hand commenting on all the names printed on the back of the boats. A laugh was shared here and there when a funny name was spotted. Some names were very clever. They sat on a bench facing the water. He put his arm around her and kissed the top of her head. She leaned her head on his shoulder and he asked, "What time is your mom expecting you?"

"I called her after breakfast and told her I was out with you and wasn't sure what time we'd land at the house. She was fine with that and wanted me to tell you thank you for calling her yesterday and taking care of me."

"I like taking care of you," his eyes explored hers.

She leaned over and kissed him, "I like it too. I feel safe with you." He put his mouth on hers and gave her a gentle kiss. She then put her head back on his shoulder. The water was calm and the sky breathtaking. They were content.

He spotted Edward waiting on the porch as he walked Karen to the door. Edward felt her forehead and seemed pleased, "No more fever?" She shook her head.

Curtis told them he needed to head on to drop off his load in the truck. Edward looked at him. He looked back at Edward. Curtis placed his hands on Karen's arms and kissed her. She kissed him back and hugged him, "I had a nice day. Thank you."

"Anytime. I'll check on you later." His gaze switched to Edward and he nodded.

Edward smiled and watched him drive away, "He's a cheeky bastard kissing you in front of me." Karen admonished him for his language, then smiled at him. "Okay, I like him. He doesn't pull his punches. He obviously loves you very much." Karen looked at Ed in surprise, "You haven't told each other that? Because I see it in your eyes when you look at him. I see it in his when he looks at you." Karen shook her head and smiled. She looked up at Ed and he gave her a hug, "It's always a nice surprise when people fall in love." He took a look at the horizon at Curtis's taillights, "He's a good man. You couldn't have chosen anyone better." She couldn't agree more. "Now, you've had a nice day out with your young man. What do you have planned for this afternoon? I have something to ask you."

Karen wasn't so sure about this. Ed had talked her into coming to the shooting range. Owen had given him the key to the building on the farm property. She stood in front of a cut out window with dividers running on each side of her. She could see a big room with a white floor and big paper targets hanging from the ceiling. Ed gave her a pair of earmuffs and eyewear for safety. He had the range bag in his hand and made sure the pistols inside the bag were unloaded.

He taught her when opening the bag to make sure the pistol was sitting in a safe direction and not pointing at anyone. He performed a safety check. Then he showed her to make sure a weapon is always pointed straight down range. He demonstrated to her how to load the weapon and pointed to the target and taught her how to fire. They spent all afternoon practicing. Ed told her they would set up weekly practices around her school schedule. He was a patient teacher. She never thought she would be handling a firearm. It was a little scary, but she liked the fact she could protect herself.

Love from Farm to Stable

Chapter 15

Curtis had a busy afternoon. He ran home to take a shower because his parents called to see if he would like to bring Karen to dinner. He remembered the conversation when he called her earlier, "My mom is making her blueberry cobbler for dessert."

"I really like her blueberry cobbler."

"Yes, I know about that sweet tooth of yours."

She could imagine him smiling over the phone, "I would love to have dinner with your family. I just need to call mom at work and tell her what I'm doing so they don't hold dinner."

He said, "I missed you this afternoon. I'm looking forward to kissing you again."

She playfully replied, "Curtis Dalton, what makes you think you're getting another kiss?"

"Maybe because of how handsome you think I am and how much you enjoyed kissing me today at the marina."

"Who said you were handsome and how do you know I enjoyed those kisses?"

"Oh, Honey. You really don't want to go there, do you?" he asked.

"You really think a lot of yourself, don't you?" she grinned.

He played along, "You could say I have a healthy respect for myself. In fact, I know you like me."

"How can you tell?"

"You spent half the day with me and now you're coming to dinner too. You must like my company."

Karen spoke up, "I like your mom's cobbler."

He returned, "I like kissing you."

She smiled and shook her head, "Okay, we've come full circle on this conversation. I'll see you in a bit. Goodbye, Curtis."

He laughed and said, "Goodbye, Karen."

A short time later, Curtis pulled up to his parents' home. She turned to him, "Do I look okay?"

He leaned over and kissed her, "What does that tell you?"

She looked at him, "Well, a 'yes' or 'no' would have been good enough."

He winked at her and said, "I like my way a whole lot better." He grinned, "Ready to go?" He came around the truck and opened her door. He took her hand to help her out of the truck and led the way into the house, "Mom? Dad? We're here."

His mom walked out of the kitchen, "Karen!" she exclaimed, as she hugged her, "I hope you don't mind hugs. I'm a big hugger."

"No, ma'am, I'm fine with that."

His mom put a hand on her forehead, "Cool as a cucumber. Good deal." Abby Dalton turned to Curtis, smoothed his hair back and asked, "How's my handsome son?"

He hugged his mom, "See Karen, Mom thinks I'm handsome." His mom looked at him with a raised eyebrow, "Never mind Mom, just a little joke between me and Karen." He smiled at Karen.

At that moment Owen walked into the kitchen. He clasped his son on the back and said, "Hey." He walked over to Karen and said, "Hi there Hon." He hugged her and felt her forehead, "Cool as a cucumber." She looked at Curtis and they smiled at each other.

"We are so glad you are joining us for dinner. Gives us somebody else pretty to look at over the table than looking at his ugly mug," he said as he pointed to his son.

"See Curtis, there is someone else that doesn't think you're handsome." She just smiled at Curtis.

His dad looked at them, "Huh?"

His wife patted his arm, "Apparently, it's a joke between these two. Are you all ready to eat? Karen, I bet you worked up an appetite this afternoon. Learning how to shoot at the gun range can be exhausting."

Curtis looked at Karen, "Gun range?"

"Yes, I didn't have a chance to tell you. Ed talked me into going to the gun range and showed me how to use a pistol. Of course, I'm just beginning. It's not as hard as I thought, but I don't know if I will ever be fully comfortable using a gun."

Everyone sat down and filled their plates. Owen glanced at Karen, "It just requires lots of practice. The biggest part about owning a gun is gun safety."

"Yes, Ed explained all that to me. It's a big responsibility. Of course, living next door to Ed growing up, Flo and I were always in and out of his house. He has a gun safe and told us the importance of being a good gun owner."

Abby shared, "Yes, we all have gun safes in our homes. It's just something we taught the kids. There are unfortunate accidents in which children are killed and it's so unnecessary if you take the right precautions."

Curtis spoke up, "If Edward's not available, let me know and I'll be happy to take you to the range."

"Thank you." She put her hand on his. He smiled at her and her green eyes sparkled with affection. Abby glanced at Owen and her husband nodded his head. His wife was catching up to figuring out Curtis and Karen had fallen in love.

Karen sat back in her chair after she finished her dinner, "Mrs. Dalton, that was probably one of the best meals I've ever had. Thank you."

"Call me, Abby please. I'm glad you enjoyed it. I love to cook and unfortunately it shows."

Karen looked at Curtis's mom and said, "I don't see where."

"Oh Honey, thank you." Abby looked at Curtis and said, "You bring her around as much as you like. Helps my ego." She smiled at Karen. They all helped clear the dishes. Abby scooped blueberry cobbler into bowls and had vanilla ice cream out on the counter ready for anyone to add to their cobbler, "How about we go into the living room for dessert? Owen has a nice fire going for us." They carried their bowls into the living room.

Karen tried her cobbler then closed her eyes, "Mmm, Abby, I meant to get the recipe from you last time. It's absolutely fabulous."

She smiled and was pleased, "I will certainly give you the recipe. It's really quite easy."

Curtis watched Karen enjoy her cobbler and thought about their day. She was much more relaxed as she carried on a conversation with his parents. He wanted to make her happy. It was that simple. When finished with dessert, Curtis helped his mom clear the bowls. Karen was looking at a painting on the wall of a small farmhouse. Owen joined her to tell her about it.

"Karen, this was the original farmhouse that belonged to my grandfather and grandmother. It actually was my great-grandfather's first, but it was passed down to my grandparents after they were married. I used to visit when I was a little thing, and they had a horse named Thunder they used to let us kids ride around the farm. They had fields all around the house and they would grow corn. We would go every summer and pick corn. We'd go to the house for lunch every Sunday and we'd shuck it and

149

my grandfather would boil the corn for our lunch. My grandmother would cook green beans and sweet potatoes. She'd also make skillet cornbread in her big black cast iron skillet. Whoo boy, that was the life."

Karen smiled at his enthusiasm and excitement during those times of his life. She asked, "What happened to the house?"

Owen said, "Progress happened. More people came to live over here and a highway was planned to go right where this house was, so they sold their land, and a highway was built there. They took their money and put it into 1,500 acres of land. We've acquired a lot more land since then. There are several buildings and crops on our land. You probably saw several today. We all have houses here. We moved the original farmhouse which we updated slightly with modern conveniences, but we were still able to keep the charm of the house intact. It's not too far from Curtis's home. My grandparents passed away some time ago, and an artist lives there now."

She looked at the farmhouse again and asked, "Do your parents live on the property too?"

He sighed, "No, Hon, they passed away. The only grandparents the kids have are Abby's folks and they live in a condo near Destin. Karen touched his arm and told him she was sorry about his parents. "I appreciate that." He patted her hand.

She gazed at the portrait," It's a pretty house."

Owen smiled and agreed, "Yes, it was in a great location before the highway came through. We had some good times there. They even filmed a movie there. A lot of people don't know that little tidbit." He smiled at her.

At that moment Curtis and his mom came back into the room. He walked up to Karen and asked, "Oh, Dad telling you about the farmhouse? It's a neat story."

"Yes," Karen said as she smiled at his father, "I didn't know about the movie. I bet that was exciting." Owen told her that his grandparents took it in stride, but the younger set always thought it was cool.

Abby interrupted and asked if anyone cared for coffee. Karen looked at her watch and said, "Oh, no ma'am. Thank you." She looked at Curtis, "I should be getting home to spend time with Mom before she goes to bed. My mother wants to know what night you'll be coming over to finish reading the book. She's ready to hear the end about Mr. Darcy and Elizabeth Bennet."

Abby exclaimed, "You're reading Pride and Prejudice? I love the movie with Colin Firth. He's incredibly good looking in that movie."

"Hon, I'm standing right here," said Owen.

"Yes, I know. A girl can still dream. I mean, Colin Firth." She sighed. Curtis and Karen smiled at his parents. Abby hugged her, "Karen, we really enjoyed dinner. We don't see our son as often as we like as he travels for the farm and has his own home. We are glad you could be here tonight. You are welcome anytime."

"Thank you again," said Karen as she headed for the front door.

Curtis hugged both of his parents and looked at them, "Thank you for everything."

His dad said, "Anytime, Son. We'll talk soon." Curtis nodded and followed Karen out of the house. He opened the truck door for her.

She turned towards him before getting into the truck, "Curtis, I want to thank you for today. Everything was…."

He interrupted her words with a kiss, "I'm sorry," he said, "I couldn't wait. You were saying?"

She gave him a sultry smile and kissed him back. When her lips left his, she said, "I think that says it all."

He kissed the top of her head and asked, "Ready?" He walked around the truck smiling. He started up the truck and they drove down the driveway.

Abby and Owen watched from the bay window as Curtis and Karen drove away. Owen put his arms around his wife. She had tears falling down her face, "It's really happened. Our son has fallen in love. It's not what he had with Marlena at all. I think when he dated Marlena, it was comfortable, and he just expected they'd get married. You can see the difference with Karen. It shows with them both." She looked up at her husband, "Do you think Curtis realizes yet that he's in love?"

"I'm not sure. But anyone watching them both could see it." He gazed at his wife's beautiful face. He was so glad she was still here. Beating cancer was tough for her along with losing their son Keith. His wife was such a fighter, and he loved her so much, "So," Owen asked,

"How about we go upstairs for the night? You can pretend I'm Colin Firth."

Abby turned to the man that she loved and kissed him, "Who needs Colin Firth when I have you?"

His mouth curved as he looked at the love in his wife's eyes. He put his arm around her as they began to climb the stairs.

Love from Farm to Stable

Chapter 16

Curtis parked his truck in front of his parents' home, grabbed the folder on the front seat and went inside, "Mom? Dad?" he called out as he shut the front door behind him.

He heard his dad call out from the kitchen, "In here."

Curtis walked into the kitchen to see his dad reading the newspaper and drinking a cup of coffee. He walked to the counter to pour himself a cup and took a look around, "Where's Mom?"

His dad said, "She's sleeping in for once."

Curtis remarked, "Guess she's worn out from last night."

His dad lifted an eyebrow as he continued reading, "Uh-huh." He smiled to himself.

Curtis continued, "You know with the big dinner and all, plus taking care of the house and everything else she does. I don't know how she gets it all done." He took a sip of his coffee, "She's like the energizer bunny."

His dad smiled and put his paper down on the table, "I won't argue with you, there Son." He joined his dad at the table. Owen put his hand on Curtis's and said, "Karen. We like her a lot. Your mother and I understand you are dating each other. She's always been a very sweet girl and it was clarified for us last night."

"Dad," Curtis interrupted.

"No, hear me out. She's gone through a lot to be so young. Her childhood was a terrible shame that a young girl should never have to go through. What happened recently to her would damage anyone." He looked at his son, "What I am saying is that you seem to understand one another. You can see it in her eyes that she loves you." He looked at his father with a question in his eyes. His dad said, "You have always been confident and sure of yourself. You haven't said anything to each other?" He shook his head.

Owen continued, "Your mom and I have always wanted you kids to make a living and to be happy. You could do your job in your sleep. Your relationship has happened quickly. We have talked to Janet because there was concern at first with the age difference." Owen held a hand up when Curtis's eyes expressed disbelief. "You had to have known what our thoughts would be as your parents. That's Janet's daughter and she has every right to look after her best interests. Don't misunderstand me, Son. We want to make sure that you see Karen as the person you want to be with, and you're not misinterpreting your feelings as being her savior or her knight in shining armor due to what has happened to her."

Curtis interrupted and gave his dad an incredulous look, "Dad, I can't believe you just said that. Are you kidding me? Her savior? Dad, if you want to know the truth about it, she's my savior. For the last 12 years I've concentrated on helping to run this farm. You remember my one big relationship I thought would last a lifetime but didn't. The other few dates I've had turned up as nothing. I lost a brother in that time as well and I thought for a time we were going to lose Mom."

He wiped the tears that he was horrified were falling down his face, especially in front of his father. His dad got up and put his hand on his shoulder, "Curtis."

"No Dad, I don't think I'm her knight in shining armor. She's more than that to me." He looked up at his father, "Do you know how broken she is inside? Do you know how hard she works to show the world a brave face? Do you know how much that must cost her at the end of the day? Yet, she gets up every day and shows up anyway for whatever has to be done."

Owen knelt down by his son's chair, so they were eye to eye, "Do you love her?"

He put his hands over his eyes to wipe his tears, "Oh, I'm crazy about her Dad. I think about her all the time. I want to be a part of her life. She trusts me. Do you know how hard it is for her to trust a man?"

His dad sat down in his chair and reached across and put his hand on his son's shoulder and said, "Well, for the other thing I wanted to say. Your mother and I taught you boys to respect women and to protect them as well, if you get my meaning."

Curtis smiled and said, "Dad, I was twelve years old when you gave me that talk. I haven't forgotten. Nothing has happened yet." His dad gave him a look. He couldn't believe he still had the power to make his children, his adult children, feel like they never could put anything past him, "Well, almost nothing has happened. How about that? Jesus, Dad, I'm over 30 years old!"

Owen replied, "And I'm your dad. That will never change." He cleared his throat and looked at his son, "One more thing I want to say." Curtis looked up at his dad and saw that moisture was filling his eyes, "You talked about earlier how you went through a lot to help this family. In looking back, I never meant for you to put your life on hold or for you to feel like you had to choose between loving someone or helping the family."

"Dad, I never minded at all. You should know that. Why would I mind helping my family? When we lost Keith, I never thought we'd survive. You and Mom set such a good example of how strong families can be. That was your son you lost and yet you and Mom still concentrated on Leslie and me, working on your grief, not to mention Mom's cancer."

Tears were rolling down his dad's face. Curtis got up and put his arms around him. A pair of arms surrounded them both. They looked up and Abby had tears running down her face as well. Her husband brushed her tears with his hand.

"Well," Abby said, "I sure do love it when my two strong men can show their emotions. I really love you both." She reached over for the tissue box and held it out to her men. Curtis sat down in his chair and watched his dad wipe his eyes with his hands.

"Abby, dear, real men don't use Kleenex."

She said, "Oh, is that so? I seemed to recall you watching a chick flick with me when we were dating, and you cried when the child's dog in the movie died. I gave you a tissue and you had no problem accepting it then."

She came around to sit on her husband's lap and he put his arm around her. "Well," Owen retorted, "I was courting you and Wally Sternum had his eye on you. You were being so nice to him. I was pulling out all the stops to keep you interested in me."

"Oh," Abby asked, "Is that what it was?"

"You're here aren't you?"

Abby leaned over to kiss her husband and replied, "Yes, I'm here." Owen kissed his wife. Then she said, "By the way, good morning."

Owen looked at his wife with love in his eyes and answered, "Good morning," and kissed his wife again.

Their son cleared his throat, "Are you guys going to kick me out again? I really would like to talk with you." His parents finished their kiss and Abby blushed as she got up to get coffee. Owen watched his wife walk to the counter. He waved his hand in his dad's face, "Uh, Dad?"

His father sighed and said, "Yes. I know you're here." Curtis smiled at his dad and Owen grinned.

Abby looked on top of the oven and remarked, "Someone made blueberry muffins too." She looked over at her husband and smiled, "Thank you." Owen winked at her. He looked at Curtis who was just staring at him.

"You finished?" he asked. Owen gazed at his wife and turned back to his eldest child.

"For now," his dad said.

Curtis looked at the folder in front of him and gave it to his dad and said, "Riley passed this to me from Detective Myers." As his dad looked at the contents of the folder, Curtis said, "This is the guy who attacked Karen. I talked to our lawyer and he sent over what he collected too."

"Son of a bitch!" His dad exclaimed.

Abby came to the table. He passed the folder to her. "Seriously?" his mom shook her head and looked angry.

Curtis was stunned, "You know who he is?

His dad looked up at him, "Clarence Higgins, the freaking third. His dad is a big power attorney with deep pockets and several judges lining those pockets. He's an ass, so I'm not surprised there's a picture of his son in here as I'm sure he's a chip off the old block."

Abby offered, "There have been rumors for years that Clarence the III hasn't been kind to the women he dates. There's never been any proof as the women wouldn't press charges." Owen looked at Abby and then at Curtis.

"What, is there something else I should know?"

Both parents were silent. His dad looked at his mother. She nodded. Owen spoke up, "You remember when Leslie worked at that pizza restaurant when she was in college?" He nodded and his dad continued, "She had a good friend who worked with her named Sunny. She was quiet, but a pretty girl. Leslie loved working with her because she did her job and was always kind to everyone who came into the restaurant. There was this guy that your sister said would always come in and sit at the friend's section where she waited tables. Sunny didn't get a good vibe from the guy. She would just take his order and bring him his food. Leslie said this guy would try to engage her in conversation, give her big tips and would ask her out. Leslie went with her to talk to the manager, and he told the girl not to worry about it. They had all kinds of customers coming into the restaurant. He said this guy was a customer and couldn't turn him away if he hadn't done anything wrong. He told her she would be safe in the building as there was always a manager there and nothing would happen to her. He would make sure of it."

Owen stopped and took a deep breath. He reached across to his wife and she held his hand. Curtis looked at his mom. Tears were running down her face. "Mom? Dad? What happened?"

Owen looked at Abby and said, "The manager's mother had been in a car wreck, so he left one of the waitresses in charge of the restaurant. In his haste to get to his mother, he forgot about what he promised Leslie's friend. Your sister wasn't working that night either, so there were only a few waitresses working. Owen pointed to the picture in the folder, "He came in towards the end of her shift. She waited on him as always as the manager told her to. Later on, the story told is that one of the waitresses overheard him ask her out and she shook her head no. He paid his bill and left the restaurant." Owen looked up at his wife, "Abby, I don't know if I can finish."

She came around the table and sat in her husband's lap, "We'll do this together, okay?" He tightened his hold on his wife. Abby took a deep breath and said, "She was walking out of the restaurant alone after her shift because the few waitresses on shift that night had several tables and couldn't take the time to walk out with her. Leslie said as she was a kindhearted girl, she hated to bother anyone. The story is that she was almost to her car, when she was attacked, dragged into the bushes where no one could see, and she was…".

Abby took a deep breath. Her son took her hand in his, "Curtis, when he was through with her, he just left her there bleeding." Abby was crying and couldn't stop the tears, "The restaurant was situated off a main street since it was a college town. She was trying to get help by flagging down one of the cars when she was hit. She was still alive and the car that hit her called an ambulance. Someone called her parents and got her to the hospital. She was able to say a few words to her parents. She knew who the man was because he always paid with a credit card and signed his name. Her parents pushed the doctors to do a full physical examination so they could have evidence they needed to press charges on their daughter's behalf." Abby looked at Owen, "I can't go on please."

Her husband pulled her to him and looked at Curtis, "She died a few hours later. The hospital notified the authorities, and a policeman was sent to pick up the evidence. When her parents tried to move forward and press charges, they were told there was no evidence found and the doctors at the hospital were reassigned. The parents didn't really know anyone as they hadn't been in the state long, but they tried to get someone to listen. They were shut down everywhere they went. Your sister came to us to see what we could do."

His dad said, "We had a few contacts we thought would do something. When those contacts would ask questions, they were shut down as well. We went to more people we thought could get something pushed through on her behalf. We were told that since there was no evidence and no witnesses, there was a very slim chance of any recourse. We found out that Clarence's dad had powerful people in place to stop any movement to get justice for Leslie's friend. Apparently, he had provided an alibi for his son which no one was going to question, at least no one that would help us or her family. Eventually her parents couldn't take the thought of staying in a place in which their daughter had basically been murdered especially with no help from the authorities, so they moved up north where they had family."

Abby looked at her son and remarked, "Your dad has a contact that we think will be a rising attorney general in the state and now your dad has contacts that have also been linked to Washington, DC. He has tried every year to talk to these contacts about reopening the case, but so far he's hit a brick wall."

Curtis looked at his parents, "It could have been Leslie."

His mother put her hand on top of his and said, "Your dad and I have thought of that very possibility every time the anniversary of her friend's death comes around. We want justice for that poor girl and death is too good for him." Owen hugged his wife tightly as Curtis saw the anger take over his mother's sadness.

Curtis glanced at his parents and said, "I want Karen safe. I'm sure the SOB is looking to take her and take me out at the same time in order to get to her. I stopped him and I'm sure that was a blow to the bastard's ego. If he didn't want anyone to know how he hurt that poor girl at the pizza restaurant, then he wouldn't have used a credit card and signed his name or gone to her table every time he ate at that restaurant, the arrogant bastard. He was standing in front of Karen at her shop, and she had a bruise on her face. The bastard hit her and there are pictures taken at the hospital as evidence. We have everyone here at the farm. It won't be too long until he figures out where she is and tries something else." His parents looked at each other.

Abby spoke up, "We see how you and Karen feel about each other."

Owen put his hand on hers, "I've already shared our concerns and how we feel."

She nodded, "It's been very quick for you, Curtis, but sometimes we can't help who we fall in love with or when it happens. We want the best for both of you. I want you to be very sure."

He looked at his mom, "I can't lose her Mom. I just found her. We need a plan."

"Okay." Abby glanced at her husband.

Owen looked at his son and his wife. He said, "I think I've come up with one.

Love from Farm to Stable

Chapter 17

Clear and warm was how the first Saturday in December arrived. Talking with his parents the night before about their plan made him feel better about protecting Karen. His parents were going to meet with Janet and Edward this morning. Curtis wanted to talk to her. She was in his thoughts, so he texted her.

"Hi. Would you like to go horseback riding today?"

"Hi, yourself. Only if I can go with a handsome man."

"You're in luck. I happen to be available." He smiled.

"I guess you'll do."

"Gee, thanks."

"Anytime." She smiled to herself. *"See you soon."*

He opened the truck door for her. His eyes held hers as she said, "Good morning."

As their lips touched, he spoke, "Good morning." He put his hands on either side of her face and deepened the kiss. She put her hands on top of his. As they pulled back from each other, Karen got into the truck and it hit her. She was in love. As Curtis walked to the door of his truck, he slowed his steps. His smile spread to his eyes and he felt truly happy. He was in love with her. He opened the truck door and looked at his future. As they drove to the stables, he glanced at her, "The radio's yours if you want to listen to music." She turned on the radio and country music blasted from it. Curtis quickly turned it down and said, "Sorry."

He could feel her looking at him. She said, "Well, just figures that someone that went to THAT school would be listening to country music." He looked over at her and saw the challenge in her eyes.

"Hey, don't knock my country music. It's the greatest kind of music in the world. Don't you know that country music has some of the best singers.... George Strait, Willie Nelson, Johnny Cash...."

"Huh, next you'll be telling me you like Dolly Parton."

"Now you've done it," he said. "Don't go saying anything mean about Dolly. She's a National Treasure."

"I see. So, you like her for her singing, is that what you're telling me?"

He glanced at her, "Now, what other reason besides her God given talent would I have for liking Dolly?" She looked out the window and started laughing. He smiled and looked at her, "Ever been on a horse before?"

Karen smiled and said, "Once. I went on a field trip in Elementary School to a local farm. The farmer there had a real gentle horse that he let all of us kids take a turn on as he led us around a circle." She shrugged, "Other than that, no, I haven't."

He pulled up to the stables, "No time like the present to learn." As he opened her door, his sister met them inside. Curtis greeted her, "Hey, Brat."

"Nice, Curtis. What a way to speak to your sister, Jerk." They grinned at each other.

Karen gazed at them both, "You two must really have a good relationship, huh?" She told Karen that since he was the eldest, she had to keep him in line.

He looked at Karen and said, "I just let her think that she has a hand in my life. She was such a brat to me and Keith. Always following us around the farm." He looked at his sister and said to Karen, "One time when Keith and I were teenagers, we got a couple of cigarettes from some friends and thought we'd be smart and smoke them in the hay barn. Leslie caught us and told Mom and Dad. Oh, after our dad was through with handing out the discipline, we got a big lecture on what would have happened if we had caught the barn on fire, not to mention the staff we have that would have lost their livelihood or harming the animals. Dad was livid. He really hammered the point home, and we never did that again." Curtis kept talking, "Of course, Keith took it the hardest. He was tough on the outside, but he had a big heart. He never liked disappointing our parents, especially Mom." Curtis and Leslie were quiet and lost in their thoughts.

Karen looked at both of them and said, "Florence was very much in love with your brother. When he would come to pick her up to go to the movies or to go get something to eat, sometimes he would invite me to come with them. I remember how nice that was that someone would let a little sister tag along."

At that moment, Leslie walked over to Karen and gave her a big hug and said, "Thank you for that. We miss him every day." She wiped the tears from her eyes, "Ahh Curtis," she sighed. Her brother came over and gave his sister a big hug. Then she socked him in his arm.

"Hey, what was that for?" asked Curtis as he rubbed his arm.

"Oh, nothing," She winked at Karen, "Just keeping you in line." She looked around and said, "Okay, kids. The horses are ready for you. I have to run."

Karen looked at her, "You're not riding with us?"

"No, I wouldn't want to intrude or have to witness all of the long looks my brother keeps giving you. I'd hate to be a third wheel."

"You wouldn't be a third wheel," said Karen.

"Yes, she would," he muttered.

She stuck her tongue out at her brother, "You're sweet, Karen. Too sweet for my brother. Maybe some of your niceness will rub off on him. Bye Jerk."

"Bye Brat."

When they walked up to the horses, Curtis saw that Leslie had picked out a gentle, sweet horse for Karen. "Oh, he's beautiful. What's his name?"

He looked at the horse and smirked, "His name is Baldwin."

"Like in Baldwin County?"

"No," he supplied, "like in the Baldwin brothers. When my sister was a teenager, she and mom used to watch movies with the Baldwin brothers. You know the phrase, "He's such a Baldwin?" She smiled and nodded her head. "That's who he's named after." Then he rolled his eyes.

She looked at Curtis's horse, "Who's he named after?"

"His name is Colonel Potter, you know, from MASH?" Karen nodded her head. "Dad was a big fan of MASH and since Colonel Potter had a horse, that's what he named him." He had packed a small bag with sandwiches and water bottles that he secured on the saddle. He gave Karen a boost up on Baldwin, then he swung up on his horse, "Ready?" Curtis asked. She nodded and followed his lead.

As they rode around the farm, they talked about their lives growing up, college experiences, work, and family. She asked him, "What about girlfriends? Have you ever thought about getting married?"

He looked at her and answered, "Well, I had a girlfriend all through college. Her name was Marlena. Our families have known each other for years. They own a big farm right down the road. I thought we were serious and naturally thought we'd settle down." Curtis looked out over the fields.

"What happened?"

"Well," he said, "Mom got diagnosed with cancer and the treatments were rough on her. I started spending a lot of time helping Dad around the farm and taking turns driving Mom to her treatments. My girlfriend wanted more of my time. She got impatient that we couldn't go out more or spend Saturdays at the beach. She was sad that my mom had cancer, but at the time she wanted the focus to be on her, and I just couldn't spare that much time with the situation going on at home."

Karen looked at him, "If you two had known each other all your lives and dated all through college, why didn't she offer to drive your mom to treatments or run errands for your family?"

He looked at her, "See, you get it. If she had truly been in love with me and wanted us to have a future, she really wasn't showing her support for what we were going through. So, it made me think that if she wasn't invested in my family at that time, then maybe we didn't want the same things for the future. I will admit what we went through would be a lot for someone to share the burden with, but I thought we loved each other, and she would support me. I don't know. Maybe it was too much to ask of someone, but at the time I didn't think so."

Karen thought about what he was saying and told him, "Don't beat yourself up rethinking your decisions. You did what your family needed you to do at the time. It sounds like your girlfriend wasn't a good fit for you after all." She asked him, "Did you date anyone after that?"

"Mom slowly got better and went into remission. I went out with a few girls whose families were friends with my family, but nothing serious. I was jealous of what Keith and your sister had as they seemed so in sync with each other, and both knew what they wanted for the future. I wanted a soulmate." He gazed at her, "I thought it would never happen for me."

Her eyes filled with understanding. They stopped their horses at a covered pavilion on the property. He secured their horses while she set out the sandwiches and water on one of the tables under the pavilion. "This is nice," Karen said as she looked around. There were picnic tables, rocking chairs and a grill.

Curtis explained to her that his grandparents had built this place for a shelter if staff or family was out here working, riding or if the weather turned bad, "My dad used to bring my mother out here just for solitude when she was recovering. They'd bring a picnic, games, or books. Sometimes we would join them, but many times it was just Dad and Mom out here. Let me show you something." He walked with her to the edge of the pavilion.

"Oh, how beautiful." She looked at the vast open fields that seemed to never end.

He agreed, "It's a nice view."

She looked up at him, "Yes, I like what I see too." She stepped closer to Curtis, "I'd like to kiss you."

He looked at her, cupped her face in his hand and asked, "Would you now?"

She smiled at him, "Yes, I want to kiss you very much, and I'd like you to kiss me back."

He moved closer to her and said, "Well, Miss Smith, I think we can make that happen."

Karen put her arms around his neck and asked, "Do you now?"

"Yes ma'am," Curtis gazed at Karen, smiled and then his lips met hers. He deepened the kiss and splayed his hands on her back and held on. They came up for air at the same time. He cleared his throat and said to her, "Well, that was nice." He had a twinkle in his eyes.

"Just nice, huh?" asked Karen, "You know," she said, "an ice cream in the summer is nice, flowers in the springtime are nice and Christmas presents are nice, but my kiss was more than nice, Curtis Dalton."

He grinned at her. "How about we have those sandwiches, and you can try to convince me again after lunch?"

"You'd be lucky if I'd want to kiss you again."

Curtis touched her cheek and remarked, "Yes, I'd be one lucky man." She smiled and handed him a sandwich.

Florence Simmons rolled over in bed and looked at her sleeping husband. She poked his arm, "Riley?"

He opened those gorgeous blue eyes and said, "Florence, if you want to go another round, you'll have to give me 5 minutes." Then he smiled at his wife. Florence hit him in the face with a pillow. "Hey!" he said in surprise as rolled over towards his wife. They smiled at each other.

Riley lowered his head and kissed her, "Have I told you today how much I love you?"

Well," she said, "We've only been awake for about 5 minutes. You can say it again if you want."

"Florence Simmons, I love you with all of my heart and I don't think that's going to change anytime soon."

"It better not," she said. "I just got my luggage monogrammed." She smiled up at her husband.

He said, "You can be such a smartass," but he smiled. Riley propped his head up on his hand. "What's got you up this early? What's bothering you?"

He knew her so well, she thought, "It's Karen. I'm worried about her."

Riley said, "Well, it's understandable with what she went through and now she's got to worry about what that SOB will try to do next. I talked to Drew Myers and he said he will keep me up to date if he hears of any movement. Also, we're supposed to be meeting at your mom's place at the farm tomorrow to talk about a plan to bring this to an end."

"That's a big part of it, but I'm still concerned about Karen and Curtis's relationship. It's happened so fast. I believe that it will turn out all right for them because I think they love each other. If I would have picked anyone for my sister, it would be someone like Curtis." She glanced at Riley, "What if I'm wrong?"

"You're not wrong. I have a good feeling about them." His wife chewed her fingernail.

Riley looked at the clock on the bedside table, "Why don't we sleep on it and talk about it more in the morning. It's barely 4 AM."

"I can't sleep Riley. My mind is going a mile a minute."

"Florence, before you met me, what did you used to do when you couldn't sleep?"

She looked at her husband and said, "I'd drink a glass of warm milk."

Riley moved closer to his wife and said, "Oh, Florence, I've got something so much better than that."

She snuggled with her husband and said, "You do huh?"

Her husband kissed her and said, "Mmm hmm." She answered his kiss with hers and settled in for the rest of the night.

Chapter 18

Sunday was for going to church and catching up with family and friends. This Sunday everyone decided to meet at the Dalton farm after church. Instead, Riley and Florence took it upon themselves and asked if everyone would like to meet at the theme park. There would be a tour of the park and lunch would be provided. All the families agreed. Detective Drew Myers and Toni McGregor would meet them at the park. For safety, the family arrived in a caravan of trucks and cars. Riley and his security team met them at the gates.

The family toured each section of the park, finally arriving at the Founding Farmers area. Riley was explaining to the group how this area was introduced to the park by his dad and uncle. Karen's gaze fell on Curtis, who was listening intently to Riley. She had a great time riding horses with him on Saturday. Now that Karen was out at the park, she felt exposed. She knew that it would be almost impossible for Clarence Higgins III to come after her here. She was surrounded by family and after Florence got hurt here a few months ago, Riley had increased his security team.

Karen shifted and her mom put her arm around her. "You okay?" Janet asked. Her daughter looked around and spotted the children's area. It would be close enough to the families to still feel safe.

She hugged her mom back and replied, "Yes, if you don't mind, I need to walk." She pointed to the area where children were playing in the farming playground.

"Want me to come with you?" Janet looked at Edward and then back to Karen.

"No ma'am. I'll be right back." She walked over to a bench by the playground and watched the children playing and climbing all over a pretend tractor, swinging on tire swings and playing a cornhole game. She wanted her life to go back to normal, or what was considered normal for her. She hadn't been back to work yet. Her boss had checked in with her every day to see how she was doing and assured her she had a job waiting if she felt like coming back.

She had added a walk-up-window to the front of the coffee shop to limit customers inside the store. This way she might feel safer, but her boss understood if Karen felt she couldn't return. Candace was still there guarding the patrons and employees. Karen sighed. She loved the coffee shop but didn't know what to do. She had talked to Florence about it, and she assured her sister that she would be there for her if she wanted to return to work.

Then there was Curtis. There were not many men she trusted like him. Oh, she had Ed, Riley and even Hunt had become a friend, but Curtis had truly become her soulmate. She heard what he said yesterday about never thinking he'd find one. Then he had looked at her.

Even though she had been distracted at the farm, she was struggling with thoughts of being attacked again. She even thought about the therapist the detective had suggested. Karen thought she might call that number tomorrow. As she continued to watch the children playing, she had come to the conclusion that it was time to get her life back together. She looked down as she clasped her hands together. She wasn't going to cower anymore. She mentally ticked off her list in her head in no certain order of importance: work, therapist, school, friends, family and Curtis. She raised her head and there he was.

He sat down next to her and held her hand. They sat quietly and watched the children playing in the farming play area. Curtis looked at the kids on the tire swings and said, "When we were kids, Leslie, Keith and I had a tire swing on the farm that Dad had hung up on one of the big tree branches. My brother and I would swing for hours. We were small enough, skin and bones really, that sometimes we could fit the two of us in there. Our sister just liked to bother us, and we really just ignored her, just for the fun of it."

Karen smiled. He let go of her hand, shifted on the bench and put his arm around her. He continued to watch the children on the swings, "One day, she decided to get even. Keith and I were swinging as usual. We were ignoring her, so she dared us to take turns to see if we could dive through the tire and land on the other side. She told us she'd hold the tire."

"Uh oh," Karen said, "and you believed her?" She started laughing.

"We knew it all back then. We were going to show her." Curtis laughed, "Yeah, it was like the classic Lucy holding the football for Charlie Brown. Keith went first and smacked right into the tire when Leslie moved it to the side when he was aiming for the middle." Karen started laughing. "Wait, that's not the best one yet," he said, "then it was my turn. I wasn't going to fall for her tricks. I saw her holding the tire and got a running start. Leslie went to move the tire and I put my shoulder into it, the tire smacked her in the face, and she fell down holding her eye." She ran crying to our parents, yelling, "Look what Curtis did, look what Curtis did!"

Karen smiled and said, "That's awful hurting your sister that way."

"Me? She was a holy terror. She deserved it."

Karen turned to face him, "So, what did your parents do?"

"I got the spanking of my life and Leslie got to spend endless hours in the tire swing."

"So," she casually remarked, "What did you do to get back at her?"

"Who, me? Why would you think I would do anything to get back at her?" Karen looked at Curtis and waited. "I took a big water balloon and situated it in a box and taped the lid. I told my sister I was sorry for the tire

giving her a black eye and gave her the box. I told her there
was a very small gift inside and she had to hold it up to
her face to see it. She looked at me but shrugged. I made it
so when she opened it, the tape would catch the balloon.
It exploded in her face." Curtis laughed, "Oh, it was the
best. She was drenched. I can't believe she fell for it."

She pinched his arm. "Ow, now what was that for?"

"You, the oldest picking on your little sister. I hope
she got you back."

He smiled, "Yeah, I went to take a shower that night
and when I went to rinse my hair, thick colored water ran
down my face. She had put food coloring in my shampoo,
and it was all over me."

Karen laughed at that, "Oh, that was a good one."

"Yeah, we kept going back and forth for a while
pranking each other until we got bored. Mom and Dad
were never so glad when we stopped. We were so
annoying."

At that point Leslie and their parents walked up and
looked at the playground. Leslie bumped Curtis with her
elbow, "Look, tire swings!" Their parents just rolled their
eyes. At that point, Riley, Florence, Edward and Janet
walked up to the group.

Curtis looked at Riley and asked, "You don't have
any water balloons, do you?"

He looked questionably at Curtis, "Who are you
planning to hit?"

Curtis looked at his sister who said, "Ha ha ha Curtis. You wouldn't be able to hit me because you throw like a girl!"

He returned, "Doesn't say much about you, then does it?" He laughed.

Owen sighed and asked, "Children, can we behave?" All the "children" in the group just grinned.

The parents looked at each other and Janet said, "Heaven help us."

Florence smiled and spoke up, "Riley has a table reserved for us at the restaurant, *Hay There*, if you are all ready for lunch." As the group filed into the restaurant, Florence looked at her husband and asked, "Is your mom able to make it with Aunt Alice?"

He answered, "No, they had a doctor visit."

She grabbed his arm and asked, "Everything okay?"

He laid his hand on her arm, "Yes, everything is fine. Just a checkup." He hugged his wife. He saw the doors open and went to greet Toni and Drew. The Daltons looked around at all of the old farm equipment attached to the walls and paintings of farms. The tables were covered with red checkered tablecloths. Antique furniture lined the walls with different farm themed objects such as roosters and tractors. They also noticed a sign that said **County Farm Museum** with an arrow pointing to a door.

Edward spoke up and said, "I'd love to see the museum. My father actually had a farm in Mississippi in the 50's and 60's. He had about 60 acres. It was destroyed during Hurricane Camille."

182

Owen said, "I'd love to see pictures of that. I have friends who have farms in Mississippi. It's a pretty drive."

Edward replied, "Yes, it is."

Riley spoke up and introduced Toni and Detective Myers to the group. After everyone had been greeted, he asked, "How about we have our lunch and then we can all tour the museum?" He looked at Curtis, "It's a special place." All of the food came on big platters, family style, so everyone could try a little bit of everything. There were platters of fried chicken, sweet potato casserole, fresh vegetables, and salad. There was a choice of 2 desserts: blueberry cobbler and a fresh fruit compote.

"Wow," Leslie exclaimed, "I'm so glad I worked out this week!"

Florence and Toni exchanged glances. Florence said, "Yes, since Toni and I have been taking spin classes here, I feel we can enjoy our lunch." Toni grinned. Everyone talked and enjoyed the food. Owen and Abby were seated by Edward and Janet, so they conversed about farm life, work and raising children. Edward talked about his time as a police officer and shared training stories with Drew. Janet talked about raising her girls and how proud she was of them. Karen and Florence looked at each other and smiled. Toni talked about her daughter, Victoria, or Tori for short. Riley asked Toni when they were going to see her again. She explained that her daughter had been terribly busy getting an organization for Autism off the ground.

Leslie was seated by Florence and Karen. They talked about Leslie's job as an interior designer. Riley and Curtis talked about the park. Curtis talked about traveling to different businesses and state conferences as part of his work for the farm. Karen looked around the table. It was so nice everyone could find something to talk about with all the different personalities and backgrounds. Her gaze landed on Curtis. He was talking to Riley about his favorite part of the park when he looked up at her. He smiled. Contentment. That's what Karen was feeling at this moment. She smiled at him. Then he looked back at Riley and continued their conversation.

When everyone had their fill of coffee and dessert, Riley cleared his throat and said, "Now would be a good time to view the museum. Looks like the lunch crowd is thinning out, so that will give you more room to move around." The group walked past the gift shop to a set of red barn doors. Riley pulled them open, and the group entered the museum. Abby and Owen walked to a wall display of colorful quilts. Janet and Edward talked with Toni about the different farm equipment displayed. The other members of the group walked to the back of the room.

Riley said to the group, "We have just added a new display behind the curtains here. There will be an official ceremony soon, but I thought you all might like to see it first. Riley looked at the Daltons, "Since you have a farm, I asked Curtis for some advice about the display. I think it's a real tribute to our farmers. Let me know what you think." He nodded at Curtis who pulled the curtain until everything displayed behind it was revealed.

Abby gasped. Owen just stared. Leslie had tears in her eyes. Karen stood by Curtis and put her hand on his arm and Florence went to hug Riley. The Daltons moved closer to the display. Above it was a black and white sketch of a barn with a silo and a windmill. The words on the plaque said, *"When someone you Love becomes a memory, that memory becomes a Treasure."* Below the plaque was framed pictures of farmers in Baldwin County whose dream was to farm and whose farms impacted the community. In the middle was a picture of Keith smiling and leaning on a tractor. Abby touched the picture of her son. Owen came up to the picture and smiled through his tears. His wife turned to him and began to cry. Curtis and Leslie both came up and put their arms around their parents.

Riley looked at Florence, who had tears streaming down her face, "Have I told you, Riley Simmons, what a wonderful man I think you are?" He looked at his wife and kissed her.

Owen looked at Curtis and said, "Thank you, I love you Son." He hugged his dad.

Abby walked up to Riley and kissed his cheek. "You could not have given us a better present, other than marrying Florence." She smiled at them and said, "We will be back to visit him often."

Leslie hugged her mom and dad. Her brother was standing beside her, "You did good, Curtis." He looked up at his sister and smiled. She hugged him. Leslie hugged Florence and Riley as well and said, "Thank you." Karen walked up to Curtis and kissed him. He put his arm around her.

Abby said, "It's a beautiful display." She looked at everyone gathered around them, "Thank you all for a wonderful day." Abby walked back up to Keith's picture and asked through her tears, "How's my handsome son?" She cried and held on to Owen as their youngest son smiled down on them.

Chapter 19

After the emotional surprise at the farmer's tribute, everyone met in the conference room at the front of the park. Owen had copies of the layout of the Dalton farm available for everyone to review. Drew talked about security on the farm. Owen shared that all their houses had security systems. He invited Drew to the farm to inspect the systems and offer advice. Cameras had been installed in certain heavily wooded areas of the farm, mostly making sure no one made it onto their property without their knowledge. Toni and Riley discussed security at the park. They would meet with staff and release Clarence's picture in case he came to the park. No one wanted to take any chances in case Karen's attacker had a plan to go after family members. Tears were falling down Karen's face. She got up and walked out of the room.

Curtis started to rise from the table and Florence put her hand on his, "Let me." She caught up with her sister in the lobby. Karen was standing with her arms folded and staring at the circus pictures on the wall. Florence put her arms around her sister. She hugged her, then cried,

"Flo, I don't want anyone hurt because of me. I don't know how I'd live with myself."

"This is not on you, Karen. This is on him." She held her sister as she cried.

Karen looked up and wiped her eyes, "The Daltons have been wonderful to me. They don't deserve this."

Florence agreed that they were a wonderful family, "There's something you need to remember about the Daltons. Through all the tragedy and hardships they have faced, they are a giving and loving family. They have no qualms with helping people. That's just who they are."

Karen nodded her head, "Yes, Curtis has been there for me every step of the way." She looked at Flo, "I know you're concerned about our relationship. Our parents even talked to each other about our age difference, but I think everyone is coming to terms with that. Flo, you have taken care of me for a long time, and I love you. It's time to trust me when it comes to Curtis. I may be young, but I know what I want. I want him."

Flo watched Karen wipe her eyes and then say, "Curtis and I have talked about our relationship and I shared with him how I have never been with another man. He understands I'm not ready for that part of our relationship and he says he's happy to wait for me. I think this is it for both of us. I can see us spending a lifetime together. I know that may sound naive and some may feel it's my age talking, but I'm settled with the knowledge that he and I love each other." Flo looked at her with a question in her eyes. Karen shook her head, "No, we haven't said the words to each other, but I know what's in our hearts."

Flo hugged her sister. She saw Curtis standing outside the doors of the conference room, "I'll head back inside and let you two have a minute." As she reached Curtis, Florence stopped and looked at him. A smile passed between them. They hugged each other, "I know you'll be good to my sister," she kissed him on the cheek, "because if you aren't, I won't have to send Riley to kick your ass. I'll do it myself."

He grinned at her and said, "I don't doubt it for a minute." Florence walked into the conference room. He moved towards the woman he loved. He touched her face where her tears had been. "Hi." he said.

"Hi, yourself."

He took her hand and put it over his heart and said, "This will always be yours and no one else's. You do understand what I'm saying? Florence told me when y'all were young, your mother used to put her hand over her heart. It would remind you and your sister how she felt about you two, how she would always take care of you and make sure you were safe. Every time you see me put my hand on my heart, you will remember how I feel about you, that I'll always take care of you and make sure you're safe."

Tears flowed from her eyes, "Just when I stopped crying, you had to start me up again." She saw what was in his eyes. He saw what was in hers. They moved together and kissed.

Curtis saw a tissue box on the lobby counter and wiped Karen's eyes, "You ready to go back in?" She nodded and they walked hand in hand back to the conference room to hear the rest of the plan. When the meeting was over, Karen and Curtis took a walk through the park, feeling safe with park security. They talked about the events of the day and passed by the Rock and Roll area and watched the riders on the roller coaster throw their arms up at a particularly fast turn and heard the screams of teenagers as the coaster dipped and came back up over the track. Soon, the Over the Moon Pavilion came into view. He picked up her hand and kissed it. She looked his way and smiled.

With a beautiful lake in the background, they took a seat on a bench. He put his arm around her. She looked at the lake with the ducks swimming and the fountain of water springing up towards the sky. She said to him, "I'm ready to go back to work." He looked at her with concern and she said, "I can't hide forever, and I've decided that I want my life back. My boss said I can start whenever I'm ready, so I want to try again. I also contacted the therapist whose name I got from the detective. She would like to meet me next week for our first conversation. Mom and Flo are going with me. I've been talking with my college advisor and he's willing to work with me so I can finish my degree." Curtis was noticeably quiet as he gazed at the calmness of the lake. Karen took a deep breath and blew it out. There was a lot to do to be back among the living. That's how she felt that she had died. Now, she was ready to live again. The man sitting next to her had a lot to do with her wanting to move on to the next adventure in her life.

Karen stared at the lake lost in her thoughts. She soon felt his hand rest on her neck and she tilted her head up. His brown eyes held kindness and he moved her head closer to his and his lips met hers. He slowly finished the kiss and whispered, "How can I help?"

Karen felt her heart fill with joy. She put her hand on his cheek and said, "Take me to work for my first day back and help me chase away my fear." He noticed the shadows that had crept into her eyes.

He turned the palm of her hand over and kissed it, "I can do that," he replied, "on one condition."

Karen raised her eyebrows and asked, "What's that?"

"That you don't mess with my coffee." His eyes twinkled and he smiled.

Love from Farm to Stable

Chapter 20

A black Infiniti pulled into a Midtown neighborhood. The man driving the car had blonde good looks and was dressed in a suit. He parked the car near a curb and looked around at the postage stamp sized houses with manicured lawns, "Ugh," he muttered, "who would live in this dump of a neighborhood? No wonder Karen is looking to move up in the world with that pretty boy rich farmer."

He looked around and zeroed in on her house. He understood the mother lived there with a retired cop. It paid to have a couple of cops in his pocket to find out information when he needed it. The house looked dark. He looked around and got out of his car. He walked up to the house. He usually could count on a chatty neighbor. Looking at the lady sitting in her rocking chair next door, he thought, "Bingo!" "Hello, I wonder if you could help me?"

The lady looked up and thought what a handsome man, "Yes, dear, what can I help you with?" she asked.

Clarence turned on the southern charm, "I'm an insurance agent and had an appointment this afternoon with the Smith family. It doesn't look like they're home." He thought about his father's advice to lay low, and he had even offered to send him out of the country for a while. He thought his father could be weak at times. Clarence wasn't going anywhere. He had every right to do what he wanted.

"Oh, dear. They aren't home, honey. They left about a week ago. I saw the older sister get in the car with Karen, Edward and Janet along with their luggage."

"Oh, well. I guess I'll just call the office and reschedule the appointment. You wouldn't happen to know where they went?"

"Oh, dearie, I went to say hello to them, thinking they were going on a trip and to see if I could take care of their mail or anything. They said they had everything taken care of. They were just going off for a little vacation. I didn't find out where."

Clarence was seething inside. He didn't dare let it show, "Well, ma'am, thank you for your time."

"Oh, there was one more thing," the old lady offered. He turned to face her. "When they were getting in the car, I heard someone talk about directions. As the car doors were about to close, I heard someone mention a farm."

Clarence smiled at the lady and nodded his head. He had them both in his sights now. He was a Higgins, and no one said "no" to him. There'd be a time when she wasn't always going to have people or her farmer watching. Never knew when a barn might catch on fire or someone would be "accidentally" hit by a car. Everybody usually came running then. He would have his chance when everyone else was distracted. Then once he got what he wanted, he might have to go a little further with his plan. He couldn't have any witnesses. He knew how to get rid of people and no one would be the wiser. He would see if Marlena came through for him with the boyfriend. If she couldn't get the job done, then he had no use for her either. Clarence Higgins III had it all. As he drove away, his thought was that he was going to keep it that way.

Love from Farm to Stable

Chapter 21

Tuesday morning dawned bright and early. Curtis walked up the steps to the house to pick up Karen for work. "Hi," she said as she leaned in and kissed him.

"Hi yourself," he smiled as he returned the kiss, "Ready?" He looked up and noticed her mom and Edward standing at the window waving to her. He nodded.

She blew a kiss to them and waved, "Are you sure this is not interfering with your schedule?"

"Yes, I'm missing out on the latest farm report. I'm also missing out on my second cup of coffee." He opened the truck door for her, "I'm joking with you. My schedule's fine."

As she passed him, she stopped, looked into his eyes, and said, "I can't do anything about the farm report, but I happen to know a great barista that can help you with that coffee."

"Will it come with a doughnut?" He gave her a teasing look, "I missed breakfast."

She walked to him and he pulled her in for a hug as she said, "Yes, a doughnut and a kiss." She felt safe as he wrapped his arms around her. They hadn't said the words to each other, but she knew what was in their hearts. She raised her head as he gazed at her with love in his eyes. Her breath caught in anticipation as she watched him close his eyes and lower his mouth to hers. As her mouth moved with his, the sensation of being loved filled her with happiness. His mouth then moved to give her a gentle kiss on the corner of her mouth. Then he pulled her in close and they held one another. They moved from each other's arms and she climbed into the truck. He made his way to the other side and slid into his seat. His eyes met hers and he smiled.

Karen was in her element. She was so glad to be back at the shop. Business was brisk now that there was a to-go window and limited seating in the shop itself so that she wouldn't feel like she was stepping back into her nightmare. Curtis had escorted her into the coffee shop that morning. He sat at a back table sipping his coffee and for a time had watched all the customers come and go. He had his laptop with him for his work. She and the second barista had a steady stream of customers, especially those searching for a mid-morning shot of caffeine. Candace sat at her desk going over paperwork. Her weapon was hidden in a secure holder on her back covered by a jacket.

Karen was busy throughout the morning serving customers at the take-out window. When she would look up and see Curtis sitting at the back table, she was comforted by his presence. So, when she looked up again, she was disappointed to see the back table empty. She knew he was terribly busy running the farm. She had to be realistic and couldn't expect him to shortchange his work to be with her 24/7. She knew that returning to work was a big step for her.

She always considered herself to be independent. She hoped her therapy sessions would help her. Karen was so lost in her thoughts; she didn't realize until she looked up that there were customers standing at her counter. She smiled when she noticed Mr. and Mrs. Dalton next in line inside the shop. Since she had no one at the take-out window, she moved over so she could wait on them.

Abby said, "Hello dear. We were out in the area and a cup of your coffee sounded like a treat. What would you recommend?" She picked out a couple of choices for Curtis's mom. While she was deciding between the two coffees, Karen glanced at Owen.

He smiled at her, "I'll take a black coffee."

Her mouth curved, "Owen, are you sure I can't talk you into trying something besides black coffee?"

His eyes sparkled, "I'm really particular about my coffee. I don't let anyone touch my coffee." He pointed in Abby's direction and said, "especially her." She ignored her husband and ordered an Oatmeal Honey Latte.

She looked at him as she pointed to the flavors of coffee on the board, "You're sure I can't change your mind?"

He replied, "No, just the black coffee."

She nodded, "Now, I know who he takes after." he raised a brow and she just smiled.

Abby gazed at her, "I think we'll sit in the back and enjoy our coffees."

Karen replied, "They will be right up." As she went to the shelf to get more cups, she happened to glance out of the window and there was Curtis, leaning against his truck with his hands in his pockets. He caught her eye. She smiled and he answered with a slow tilt of his mouth. He put his hand over his heart. She put her hand over hers. He got into his truck and drove away. She finished making the drinks, plated two pieces of their famous cinnamon pecan bread, and delivered them to his parents.

Abby looked up, "Dear, what do you have here?" Karen set the coffees and the bread on the table.

She realized that Curtis's parents had become very special to her, so she said, "It's my way of saying thank you."

Owen asked, "What for Hon?"

"For being here," Karen said, "thank you for being here." She smiled at them and walked back to the counter to take the next order.

Her customers were steady for the next couple of hours. After Abby and Owen left, her mom and Ed came in for a couple of specialty coffees. They stayed for about an hour. Then, Florence and Riley popped in for two cappuccinos and a box of doughnuts for the office at the park. After visiting with each other, polishing off a doughnut each and their drinks, an hour had gone by. Karen felt so comforted by her family and friends, that she told her boss she could stay the whole day and close. She felt fine as long as someone was with her. She was glad to see Candace again and felt safe with her being on the job. Hunt brought in four salads for the staff in the shop for lunch. He ended up leaving with a nonfat latte and a brownie, which had her shaking her head and Hunt grinning at her on the way out.

The afternoon flew by with all the mundane chores to be done in a shop like this. Karen wiped her brow and went to the back to take a break. Half an hour later, Candace came through the kitchen doors and remarked, "Karen, there's a man here to see you. Nice looking guy if you ask me. Dark hair, blue eyes, great physique, serious expression. I already checked him out," she said smiling. As her smile faded, she continued, "He would like to leave some business cards here. He said he knew you from school. Since I already locked the door for the evening, he's waiting at the window." Candace walked back to her desk.

Karen walked out of the kitchen. The man had his back to her. She stopped at the take-out window, tapped on the glass, and inquired, "Hello?"

He turned and quietly asked, "Karen Smith? Do you remember me? Florence and I used to carpool together in high school. We'd pick you up sometimes and you'd go to dinner or the library with us when we had study groups."

Her eyes widened, "Wally Sternum? Oh, my goodness!" She gestured for Candace to unlock the door. When he walked in, she clasped his hands and said, "Hi! Florence won't believe this! How have you been?"

He gently removed his hands, placed them in his pockets and replied, "Doin' okay. I happened to see your local ad for the coffee shop and thought that was you. Thought I'd come by and see what your shop was all about. Maybe I could leave my business cards here."

"Sure," Karen said, "can I get you anything? I can make you a drink or offer you a pastry."

"No, thank you. How's Florence?"

"Oh, she just got married," Karen remarked as she rubbed her neck.

"A newlywed. How 'bout that?" He cleared his throat as a sad expression crossed his face, "I heard that Keith Dalton passed away a few years ago." She noticed he paused for a moment and took a deep breath, "I hated to hear that, but I'm glad she found someone to love enough to try again." He didn't say anything else.

"Yes, he's a good person and they are perfect for each other. He owns a theme park and she's the educator there."

His mouth curved slightly, "I'm really glad to catch up with you," said Wally. He happened to notice Karen continuously rub her neck. He reached into his pocket and pulled out a stack of business cards.

She took the cards and glanced at one as she put them on the top of the counter," Oh, that's a great business to be in and so helpful to those in pain."

Wally looked at her and expressed his thought out loud, "What's wrong with your neck?"

"It's been a long day. It just doesn't feel right. I'm sure I'll be fine with a long soak when I get home."

"Do you mind if I take a look?"

Karen hesitated, but remembered how nice he always was to her and respectful to her mom when he would take Flo back and forth to school. Flo had nothing but kind words to say about Wally. "Sure." Karen turned her back to him.

Curtis had finished with his business in Mobile and pulled up to the coffee shop. Florence and Riley offered to bring Karen home, but he wanted to be the one to take her home. He smiled when he thought about seeing her. He understood she had a steady stream of customers today, with many being friends and family visiting. He was glad. Curtis grabbed the bouquet of flowers off the front seat and headed into the shop. Candace saw him park his truck and had just opened the front door when he saw a man with his hands around Karen's neck. Before anyone could move, he dropped the flowers, slammed the man against the wall and held the man's arm up behind his back so he couldn't move.

Candace had her hand on her weapon, "Mr. Dalton, let him go."

Karen said, "I'm okay, let him go." Curtis was so focused on the man; the women's pleas didn't register.

Wally quietly suggested, "You're going to want to let me go."

Curtis pulled Wally's arm further up his back and uttered, "Not until you tell me why you had her hands on her neck. Is it fun for you to harass women?"

"Harass women? What the hell are you talking about? You bend my arm anymore I'm going to drop you on your ass."

Karen tried again, "It's not what you think. Let him go." He turned his gaze towards her and before he could release his grip, Wally hooked a foot around Curtis's lower leg, and he hit the floor.

Candace stood between the two men, "That's enough." Curtis promptly stood up and faced the man.

Karen came to stand in front of him with an unhappy expression on her face. She pointed to the business cards on the counter, "Wally is an old friend of Flo's. They used to carpool in high school. He was at our house all the time. He saw the coffee shop ad and thought he recognized me. He came by to say hello and ask if he could drop off his business cards. My neck has been bothering me all afternoon, so he offered to take a look. That's all."

Wally remarked to Curtis, "If you've got a problem with any of that, we can go another round. I don't take too kindly to have my hand or arm injured since I depend on those things for my livelihood."

"You keep insulting me, I might just take you up on your offer of another round."

Karen had enough. She pointed to a table in the front and stared at Curtis, "You sit in that chair there." Then she glanced at Wally and pointed to a chair at the same table, "You sit there." Both men looked at her. "Now!" she ordered. Both men scowled at each other and took a seat. She went back behind the counter, made two frozen coffee drinks, and plopped them down on their table, "Here, this should cool you both off." She locked the front door and walked to the kitchen, "I'm going to finish the last of the dishes and straighten up. Hopefully, you'll be acting like adults by the time I get back." Candace, her hands propped on her hips, waited for a minute as she surveyed both men. Satisfied they weren't going to mix it up, she returned to her station. The men sipped their drinks in silence.

Curtis got up to stretch his back and walk around the room. The security guard looked at him. He held his hands up and remarked, "I'm not going to do anything, okay?" Candace went back to writing in her notebook. Wally stretched out his arm and flexed his hand.

Curtis leaned against the counter looking around the room, "Sorry about your arm. When I saw your hands around Karen's neck, I just reacted."

Wally sat back in his chair, glanced at Curtis and blew out a breath, "You and Karen, huh?"

Curtis's gaze zeroed in on the other man, "Is there a problem?"

He held up his hands, "No problem. I've always liked Florence and her sister. They're good girls, you know what I mean? Nice, decent people who would help out anyone in a pinch." Wally looked back at the closed kitchen doors and heard the rattling of dishes. He continued, "Florence always seemed a little bit tougher. I always worried about Karen. She's a gentle person. I thought people would take advantage of her, but instead they seemed to embrace her good nature." Curtis nodded and went to sit back at the table. He sat up to stretch his back. Wally stared at him, "Back bothering you? Had to do the leg drop on you. Couldn't have you mess up my arm."

Curtis gave a quick smile and said, "I'll admit it. That was a nice move."

He smiled briefly, "Yeah, when I was little, I was all skin and bones, wore glasses too. I got picked on a lot and got sick of it. I asked my dad for self-defense lessons. He had some buddies that were military, so they would work with me in their spare time. The training stuck. So, when the little assholes at school would start in on me, I was able to shut it down. They never bothered me again." He continued, "You move pretty quick. Didn't know what hit me at first and before I knew it you had me up against the wall."

Curtis had a twinkle in his eye, "Yeah, my dad wanted to go into law enforcement when he was younger. He actually had training with all types of guns and physical defense. He was taught verbal de-escalation first before handing out the physical part. His dad got sick, and he ended up running the farm and that was that. But he did teach his children how to defend themselves. We all learned how to shoot and fight." Wally nodded.

Curtis stood up and walked around the room. "So, to go back to our earlier conversation, why was I up against the wall? "asked Wally.

Curtis looked at the kitchen door and heard the woman he loved moving around. He took a deep breath and said, "Karen was assaulted here recently. I happened to show up at the right time and broke the SOB's nose. Of course, it helped having a rifle pointed at his face. He was arrested." Curtis nodded at Candace. "The owner hired security. So, now do you understand?"

Wally's eyes narrowed, "Yes, good for you. He still rotting in jail?"

"No," replied Curtis, "he made bail the same night. Rich asshole with a rich daddy who protects his little boy. Family and friends have all been showing up here as she just started back at work today. Just trying to be supportive. We're making sure he doesn't show up again."

Wally said, "I can come by a few times. I don't mind."

He noticed Wally kept turning his wedding band around his finger and suggested, "Maybe your wife would enjoy a drink from here too." Wally was quiet for a minute and didn't respond. He stopped turning his ring. Since there was no response, Curtis continued to move around the room to stretch his back. Wally reached out one of his cards to him. He returned to his chair and read the card. He started laughing and couldn't stop.

Wally quirked an eyebrow up, "Care to let me in on what's so funny?"

Curtis asked, "You're Wally Sternum, Jr.?" He stared at Curtis. "I'm Curtis Dalton. My mom is Abby Dalton."

Wally's eyes widened, "Abby Dalton who married Owen Dalton? You're their son? Are you kidding me? My dad has pictures from college of all his friends." He whistled through his teeth, "Hey, no offense, but your mom was a looker."

"Yeah," Curtis grinned, "my dad would agree with you and tell you nothing's changed there."

Wally said, "My dad used to tell me the story about how he thought he might have a chance with your mom, but she only had eyes for your dad. He knew that at the time, but he would tell me how nice your mom was to him. I don't think your dad was very happy about that. It all worked out. My dad and mom met when he was at a conference. They're good together and still crazy about each other."

Curtis looked at the business card, "You're both chiropractors? Your last name is Sternum." Curtis smiled, "That ever trip you up with what you do?"

Wally sighed and took a sip of his drink, "It's actually great advertising." They both laughed.

At that moment, Karen came out of the kitchen and studied both men, "You two seem to have settled things." The men looked at each other and nodded.

Wally glanced at Curtis, "You have my card. You can come see me about that back." The chiropractor grabbed his coat, cleaned his table, and said to Karen, "Hey, it was good seeing you." He nodded to Curtis as he walked out the door.

She sat down across from Curtis and stared at him with her chin propped on her hand. He rubbed his hands down his face and sighed. She began, "Sounds like you two know each other."

"My parents and his dad were all in school together," he replied. She nodded and put her hands in her lap. He began, "Listen, I'm sorry. I overreacted. I thought he was hurting you," he stared at her. She was quiet. She raised her eyes to his. He still saw the love there, but there was sadness too.

"It's taken everything I have to get over what happened. I don't know if I'll ever be over it completely. You have been a major part of helping me heal. I know that and I won't ever forget what you have done for me. It's one thing when you save me from being assaulted or worse. It's another when an innocent person is trying to help me, you misunderstand and react without taking in the whole situation. Candace would have had her weapon out if there had been a problem. I went through violence when I was growing up. I won't have it in my life if I can help it. I can't go through that again. If we're going to be together, you have to understand this." She put her hand on his. He held her hand. Tears were running down her face. Candace brought over a box of tissues and touched her shoulder.

Curtis explained, "I can't be any less than what I am. I was taught to respect and protect women. After what happened here before, I wanted nothing more than to know you're safe. When I saw Wally's hands on you tonight, I reacted because that's what I do when I think someone is in trouble. Yes, I should have taken a minute and looked at the situation," he squeezed her hand, "but, it's you I'm concerned about. How about we close down the shop for the night, and I take you home?" Karen nodded. Candace told them she would turn out the lights and meet them by the door. He picked up the bouquet of flowers and handed them to her, "I will always be here for you because that's just the way it is for us."

She smelled the fragrant roses, "They're beautiful. Thank you." Candace let them out then locked the door and watched them drive away. They were a great couple. She had every confidence they would work this out together.

It was a silent drive home to the farm. He glanced over at Karen, who was staring out of the window deep in thought. She was still holding the flowers. He shouldn't have acted the way he did, but it's just how he was wired. He wanted to take care of her and that meant protecting her. He felt she was miles away from him right now. Curtis waited for oncoming traffic to pass, then he turned on to the road leading to their homes. He pulled up at Karen's. He turned off the engine and waited. He felt her hand grab his. He glanced at her and saw tears in her eyes. His eyes moistened as well. This was all on him. He made her cry. He touched her cheek, "Hey, I can't apologize enough."

"Curtis, I need you to walk me to the door please." He got out of the truck and opened her door. He took her hand and kissed it. She put her hand on his cheek, "Curtis, you're one of the best men I have ever met. I'm so glad you're a part of my life. I hope you don't take this the wrong way, but I'm going to need a few days to sort some things out, okay?" He stood frozen. She saw the look on his face. She put both hands on his cheeks and touched her mouth to his. Curtis closed his eyes and savored her kiss. She looked at him, "It's going to be okay. You and I are fine. I just need some time to myself. I know you understand me." He pulled her to him and held her tight. He smoothed her hair with his hand. Curtis let her go and nodded. He watched her walk inside. She turned at the door with tears in her eyes and put her hand on her heart. He slowly raised his hand to cover his heart. She closed the door behind her.

Curtis felt as if his world just shattered. He took a deep breath and walked to his truck. His hand was on the handle. She said they were fine. He did understand her. He really did. So why did he feel that something had shifted? He looked down the road and didn't feel like going home. He needed to talk to someone. He got into the truck and soon pulled up at his parents' house. He saw the light was on in the kitchen.

As he walked up the steps, his dad opened the door, "Curtis?" He didn't care that he was over 30. He didn't care that he was supposed to take this like a man. He walked straight into his father's arms. His dad held on to his son, "Curtis, what's happened?"

He looked at his dad, "Can we talk, Dad?"

"Sure, come on in. We're just finishing up in the kitchen."

Curtis walked into the kitchen. His mom turned around to tell him hello and saw his face, "Curtis, what's wrong?" She walked up to him and hugged him. Ever since he was little, his mom's hugs always seemed to make things right. He wasn't so sure this time.

"I wanted to talk to Dad, if that's all right."

"Sure, honey," She looked at Owen, "I'll be in the living room if you need me." She touched her husband's arm, and he patted her hand.

"Have you had dinner, Son? I could fix you something."

"I'm not hungry, Dad. I just wanted to talk."

"Have a seat." Owen poured two cups of coffee and set one down in front of his son.

"Thanks, Dad." He cleared his throat, "I did something stupid tonight." He looked at his father, "I went to the shop to take Karen home. I wanted her first day back at work to be special, so I bought her some flowers on my way there. I had them in my hand and

Candace was opening the door for me. I saw a man with his hands around Karen's neck and I just reacted." He put his hands around the coffee cup. His dad waited. Curtis said, "I had him pinned to the wall before I even knew what was happening. Karen begged me to let him go, that it wasn't what I thought. I just saw red, Dad. I didn't want anyone else to hurt her."

"Who is he, Son?"

"He was someone Florence had gone to school with, and Karen knew him from that time. He has a business with his father now. He had seen the coffee shop advertisement in the local magazine and recognized her. The guy wanted to see her and brought business cards with him for her to display in the shop." Curtis sipped his coffee, "Karen and Candace kept telling me to let him go. By the time it registered that he was not there to hurt her, he had hooked his foot around my leg and before I knew it, I was on the floor."

Owen sipped his coffee and made a remark, "Sounds like he's had some training in defense tactics."

"Yes," he smiled, "Karen told us in no uncertain terms to sit down at a table while she went back to clean the kitchen. She gave us a couple of drinks and told us when she came back into the room, we better be acting like adults."

Owen's mouth curved, "Sounds like something your mother would say."

"The guy and I talked it out, but she wasn't so forgiving. After he left, she talked to me about how she won't live with violence after the life she had with her uncle. She can't have me overreacting and threatening people when I don't understand the situation."

His father put his hand on Curtis's, "What happened after that?"

His eyes moistened, "I drove her home. We didn't say anything the whole time in the truck. Karen asked me to walk her to her door. She told me she wanted a few days to herself to sort some things out." He looked at his dad, "She promised me we were fine, that she just needed some time to herself. She told me that since I understood her, it would all be okay. It doesn't feel okay, Dad. I love her. I don't want to lose her."

"Have you told Karen how you feel about her?"

"I haven't said the words Dad, but she knows."

"Curtis, women need to hear the words. When I was dating your mom, it was hard for me to tell her my feelings. I grew up learning you didn't need to talk about something, you just did what was expected. So, your mom had to pull a lot of that out of me. I thought she knew how I felt, even though I didn't say it. I was wrong. She was patient with me, and I thank my lucky stars for her every day." He looked at Curtis and cleared his throat, "Son, I was patient with her too. We loved each other. She wasn't quite ready to give herself to me completely, so we waited until we were married." He smiled at his son, "It was a nice honeymoon."

"Um, Dad. That's okay. There are some things I don't need to hear."

"Curtis, we men act stupid on occasion. That doesn't mean those who are close to us won't eventually forgive us. That's what love is. It's give and take. It's learning each other's strengths and weaknesses. It's living through the hard times together. It's not walking away when someone needs time."

Curtis sipped his coffee and nodded, "You're kind of smart for an old man."

"Yeah, well. I'm sorry my intelligence didn't get passed down to you." His dad's eyes crinkled. Curtis smiled. His dad asked, "So, who was this guy who took you down to the floor? I thought I taught you better than that."

"You won't believe who took me down. It's kind of funny, actually."

"Why's it funny?" Curtis fished the business card out of his pocket and set it down in front of his dad. He glanced at the card and then did a double take. He looked up at his son, who had a big grin on his face. Owen looked at the card again and yelled for his wife, "Abby Dalton, get in here!"

Love from Farm to Stable

Chapter 22

C urtis worked extremely hard around the farm to keep his mind occupied. It would be Christmas soon. He just didn't feel like celebrating anything, much less a holiday. He checked in with staff, helped with the horses and met with other farmers. He mucked out the stalls, cleaned his house and even had dinner with his parents when he found the time. Reminders of Karen were everywhere. He thought he smelled her scent in his truck. She had left her JAGS hat in his back seat. He kept it on the seat as a reminder of her gentleness, her goodness and her smile. He missed her.

By Friday, he had settled in a routine. He worked, traveled, and then came home to an empty house. Karen wasn't there to ask him to take her to work, to smile at him or to kiss him. Friday afternoon, he was driving around the farm when he got a text from his dad to come by the house. Someone was there to see him. Leave it up to his dad to be cryptic. Maybe Karen had missed him and wanted to see him. He could only hope. He turned into his parents' driveway and parked by the steps. He got out of the truck and greeted the person sitting on the steps, "Florence."

"Hi Curtis," Florence said as she hugged her jacket around her.

"Why don't we go inside so you don't freeze, and Riley won't come after me for causing you to catch pneumonia?"

"I already talked with your parents. I wanted to talk to you."

"Come on, let's go into the kitchen, we can have coffee and talk." She nodded. He led her into the kitchen. His parents were nowhere to be found. They were good like that to give people space when it was needed. He poured them coffee, put out sugar, cream and sat down across from Florence. He was quiet and waited.

She stirred sugar and cream into her coffee then put her spoon on her saucer, "I wanted to talk about you and my sister." She glanced at him. She used to be so comforted by his warm, kind brown eyes, which looked vacant now. She took a breath and asked, "Have you heard from her?" He remained quiet. Florence continued, "She called me crying and told me what happened with Wally at the shop." She placed her hand on the table and he put his hand in hers, "I understand you were trying to protect her. I know you love her. I don't think either of you have said the words yet, but I know what I see. You know why she's having difficulty with what happened with you and Wally at the shop. I know you understand our background. She just needs some time."

Tears were streaming down her face. Florence took a tissue Curtis offered her and continued talking, "She's such an amazing sister. I have been so fortunate to have her, and I am so sad that such a sweet person has had such a run of horrible experiences in her life." Florence added, "She goes to work and school. We go to the therapist with her. That's her life right now. She's quiet and rarely speaks to anyone except when she has to speak. She's working some things out in her head, but I miss her, Curtis. You understand what I mean. I miss her light and her sense of humor. I miss her smile." He cleared his throat, folded his hands on the table and shifted in his seat. She put her hand on top of his, "My sister so lost without you. She doesn't say so, but I can tell."

He felt the moisture gather in his eyes. He blinked back his sadness. He cleared his throat, "What do you expect me to do, Florence? She wanted space and I decided to give that to her. Has she asked for me?" Florence sighed and shook her head.

She got to her feet and he stood as well. She handed him a card, "This is an invitation to the Christmas Country Hoedown at the park tomorrow night. It's a fundraiser. The whole family is going, including Karen. We are making her go. She didn't want to, but we put our foot down. Your family, my family and a few family friends will be there." She put her hand on his shoulder and kissed his cheek, "I love you, Curtis. You are truly the brother I never had and I'm grateful to have you in my life."

Curtis gazed at her and squeezed her hand, "I love you too kiddo."

She motioned towards the card she had given him, "Think about it. I hope to see you there." She left him in the kitchen as she made her way to the front door. The Daltons were coming in from a walk. She hugged them both and then crossed her fingers. They did the same.

It was Saturday, and Karen was running on autopilot. The coffee shop had a steady stream of customers taking a break from early shopping. Christmas would be here soon. Customers bought several pans of the orange and cranberry loaves that were popular this time of year. Many people would freeze the extra loaves to have on hand throughout the next few months. She smiled at the customers as she handed over their orders. She continued to smile throughout the day, even though she was hollow inside. Karen went through the motions of her life. She had officially finished school and all of the components she needed for her degree. She was hoping to be working in a hospital or clinic soon. She had talked to Hunt about his experience with Speech Language Pathologists and had a couple of leads.

Life was lonely. She missed Curtis so much sometimes she felt she couldn't breathe. She hadn't been sleeping well. The nightmares had returned, but she hadn't shared that with anyone. Florence had taken her to the park to spend time with them and sometimes Hunt would join them for dinner. But she lived in fear that the man would return. She felt this time, he would go further than just hitting her. He had a lesson to teach her and Curtis. She worried about Curtis getting hurt on her behalf. That kept her up nights more than worrying about her own safety. Ed had continued to work with her at the shooting range. She was getting more comfortable using a pistol. She just hoped she never had to fire one.

Her thoughts turned to tonight. It was the Christmas Country Hoedown at the park. She would rather stay home than have to put on a smile and be around a crowd of people. But she would show up for Florence. Her sister was worried about her. Her mom was worried about her not really wanting to talk at home. She just didn't have the energy. Karen's reflections were interrupted by the laughter of children. She looked over at the families enjoying their time together eating the special gingerbread cookies her boss had provided for the shop. Curtis came to mind. He would make a great father one day. He was funny, patient, and kind.

She wondered what her life would have been like if she had been given a father such as Ed, who lost his little girl when she was young. Ed had saved her family. She had come to know Curtis's family and enjoyed being around them. Karen began to wipe down tables and collected plates and cups. She didn't know how she was going to handle seeing him tonight if he decided to attend the festivities. She didn't want to ask Florence if he was going to be there. Her eyes moistened. If she was honest with herself, she should have reached out to him. He had given her the time she asked for and she wanted a lifetime with him. She just didn't know how to get out of her own way to make it happen.

Chapter 23

Dusk had fallen. The Hospitality Center at the Jubilee Sunset Theme Park was bustling with crowds of guests dressed in all manner of outfits. Christmas sweaters, dresses, jeans, and boots seemed to be the theme for the evening. Guests were line dancing or two-stepping to music provided by a local country band.

Karen sat with her family. She was dressed in a crisp white shirt, jeans and to satisfy Florence, a pair of black boots. Florence had brushed out her long hair and applied make-up for her. Hunt had arrived earlier wearing a Christmas sweater with a reindeer design on the front with a red nose blinking in the middle of its face. He smiled at her and told her he had just come from the afternoon Christmas party Riley had set up for the children on the main street in the park. She smiled at him. It was a true smile for once. Leave it to Hunt.

The Daltons had joined them at their table. Abby, Owen and Leslie sat next to her mom and Edward. Toni had brought her daughter, Tori. Drew Myers was sitting at their table as well. Abby had even reached out to the Sternums. She had called the number on Wally's business card and invited them to the hoedown. They sat across from Abby and Owen. There was no sign of Curtis. Karen tried not to show her disappointment. Everyone made small talk. Florence and Riley got up to join in a line dance. Hunt asked Karen if she'd like to dance but she declined. Leslie joined Hunt on the dance floor. Karen looked around at all of the guests. Many families were seated together. Business groups with their logos displayed took up many of the tables. A dozen women laughed and carried on at their table decorated with a retirement centerpiece. Karen thought the women looked familiar. It looked like it was a successful night. A portion of the proceeds went to charity.

She heard the Daltons talking across from her. She saw them look towards the entrance and Abby said, "There he is." Curtis was walking through the door and Karen's heart dropped. He looked so handsome in a red and white checkered button-down shirt, jeans, and boots. He locked eyes with her and headed to the table. Karen sat up straight and waited for him. A woman who she had never met walked up to Curtis and stood in front of him. She put her hand on his arm and began talking to him. She was very striking with long brown hair and had a curvy figure encased in an expensive designer dress with a pair of red boots to match. Karen heard Abby gasp and ask, "What is Marlena doing here?" Owen put his arm around his wife. Abby exclaimed to her husband, "This was their chance. They don't need Marlena in the middle." They both looked back at Karen and saw that her chair was

224

empty. Owen told her he thought Curtis would make his excuses and move on. Karen's mother had seen the woman walk up to Curtis. Janet did not see her daughter. She was worried. Janet thought maybe they needed time together to talk. Leslie and Florence watched from the dance floor.

The woman Curtis had dated years ago stood in his way, "Curtis," Marlena commented, "how have you been?" She kept her hand on his arm.

He shifted his position so she had to drop her hand, "Marlena, if you will excuse me. I see my family." She stood in front of him so he couldn't pass. The sultry look she gave him was one of confidence and assurance. She didn't allow him to see the disgust for herself behind that confident look. She was broken inside. Curtis was such a good man, but she had her father to think about. She was in too deep. She touched his arm. He looked at the chair where Karen had been sitting. It was now vacant. He silently cursed Marlena and asked, "What is this all about?"

She remarked, "I just thought if you weren't seeing anyone, we might get together for old times' sake."

He replied, "Marlena, that ship sailed a long time ago. Now if you'll excuse me." She tried once more by putting her hand on his chest. She was sickened by her behavior but couldn't stop herself from touching him. This was the last good thing she had once in her life, and she had stupidly let him go. He looked down at her hand.

Leslie was fuming on the dance floor. Abby rose from her chair.

Then it happened, "Curtis, hi darling, I'm so sorry. There was such a line at the drink stand!" Karen exclaimed as she handed him a beer. She looked at the woman who had her hand on his chest, "I'm sorry, ever since Curtis and I have been together, I haven't begun to meet all of his friends." Marlena glanced at Karen and dropped her hand from his chest. She moved in Marlena's space, stood in front of Curtis, and said, 'I'm Karen and you are?"

Marlena glanced at her and then back at the man she used to date and replied, "I'm Marlena."

Karen smiled pleasantly, "How do you know each other?"

Marlena looked at the man she lost a long time ago and smirked to cover her sorrow, "We go way back, don't we?"

Karen looked up at Curtis who was looking at her with amusement and a hint of admiration. Before he could answer, Karen interrupted, "Oh, I remember now. You're Marlena. You two used to go out together, didn't you?" The other woman looked surprised. Karen moved closer to the man she was meant to be with and threaded her arm through his, "Oh, Honey, we tell each other everything. Don't be embarrassed. I'm sure we've all run into our exes from time to time." She loosened herself from Curtis and stood in front of him, "Darling, didn't you promise me a dance?"

226

Curtis cleared his throat so not to laugh and said, "Why, yes Darling, I certainly did." His eyes turned from amusement to affection. He held out his arm.

She took his arm, "Oh," she said as she took the beer from Curtis's hand and gave it to Marlena, "You don't mind holding this, do you Honey?" Marlena looked nonplussed as she held on to the beer. Karen and Curtis walked past Abby and Owen who were holding each other and grinning. Karen's mom had tears in her eyes as Edward held her. Karen passed Leslie and high fived her. Leslie and Hunt both smiled. Florence hugged her sister. Riley winked at her. He then continued walking with her until they claimed a spot on the dance floor. He took her hand in his and put his other hand on her waist. She put her hand on his shoulder. They began to move to a slow country love song.

Her bravado seemed to falter. Curtis lifted her chin, "Hey, don't stop now, you're on a roll, *Darling.*"

Karen watched him, "Are you making fun of me?"

"Never in a million years. Do you know how much I enjoyed the last 15 minutes? It was priceless. Mind telling me what got into you?"

She met his gaze, "You did." She watched his warm brown eyes fill with emotion. As they moved around the room, she spoke, "I realized that I didn't like that woman being that close to you. I didn't want her touching you."

"Why is that?" Curtis's eyes gleamed.

She replied, "Because I want to be the one who does that." Her eyes began to fill, "Because I need you.

227

Because I miss you." Her tears began to fall, "Because I want you." He pulled her in closer and held her as they moved across the dance floor.

"I missed you too," said Curtis. As they moved together, she raised her head and he continued," I need you, Karen, and I definitely want you."

"So," she held on to him and asked, "What do we do about it?"

He gave a short laugh, "Oh, Miss Smith, are you propositioning me?" As he turned with her on the dance floor, she glanced up at him and smiled. He sucked in a breath, "There it is. That smile. Do you know how absolutely beautiful you are?"

She responded, "When you look at me, you make me feel beautiful." He moved with her on the dance floor as the song changed to a song by John Michael Montgomery, "*I Love the Way You Love Me.*"

"I'm sorry for what happened at the shop. I didn't mean to cause you any more pain," Curtis apologized.

Karen looked at him, "I thought about what you said that night at the shop. I don't want you to change. Because the man you are is the man I want to be with. I just want you to make sure that you look before you leap," she smiled, "literally." His eyes crinkled with laughter.

She focused on the dancers around her and finally the song. She sighed, "I love this song. Flo and I used to go country dancing when she was in college. We had some pretty fancy moves."

Karen cut her eyes to Curtis as he spoke, "So you're telling me you want to go fancy out here to a slow song?"

Her eyes glowed and she nodded. He got into position, "You ready?" She answered by moving into position. They began to move across the dance floor with a Country Waltz then segued into a slow dance two-step. As the music built to a crescendo, they changed into a swing with turns and then with the words, *"I Love the Way You Love Me"*, he held her as she bent backwards over into a dip. When he brought her back up to meet him, they both laughed. As the song finished, they held onto each other. He smoothed her hair back from her face. She inched forward for a kiss. He touched her cheek with his thumb, then moved it down to her mouth to open her lips. He met her lips with his and they kissed.

She slowly broke the kiss and put her hand on his cheek, "Thank you for the dance."

He took her hand from his cheek and kissed her palm, "Anytime, *Darling*." he winked at her. They walked arm and arm back to the table, where their family and friends stood up and clapped.

He passed by his sister Leslie, who put her hand on his arm and muttered good naturedly, "Show-off." They both laughed.

Abby and Owen met Karen at the table. Abby moved forward and hugged her, "Thank you for saving my son, in more ways than one." Owen was standing behind Abby and winked at Karen. Abby then turned to Curtis and hugged him, "I'm so proud of you." She brushed his hair back and asked, "How is my handsome son?"

"Happy, Mom. I'm happy," he smiled.

His dad tagged him on the arm and said, "That's all we want for you."

Karen had walked over to talk with Janet and Ed. Her mom told her that she was proud of the woman she had become. She was proud of both of her daughters. Ed hugged Karen.

Florence and Riley walked up to Curtis. He glanced at her, "Is everything okay with us?" he asked.

Florence had tears in her eyes as she hugged him, "Yes, thank you so much for making my sister so happy."

"It's been quite the evening," he laughed, "especially when she came to my rescue."

Riley smiled, "Yes, it's been quite a night." He put his arm around his wife, and she smiled at him. Karen joined the group. Curtis put his arm around her. Hunt sauntered up to the group holding a bottle of water. Riley asked, "Are you on call tonight?"

"Yeah. No adult beverages for me until Christmas. I'm off for a few blessed days around that time."

Riley glanced at his best friend, "Uh Hunt, you do know your nose is blinking?"

Hunt looked down at his sweater as Leslie, Drew, Tori and even Wally joined the group. "Oh, that's not the best part." Hunt reached into his pocket. He attached a red nose over his own, "Do you know how much it costs Santa to park his sleigh?" Everyone looked at him. "Nothing, it's on the house." He glanced around the group as there was silence. He looked offended as he took off the red nose, "Now, you all have no sense of humor. The kids at the party today loved that joke!"

Riley put his hand on his best friend's back and grinned, "How about we all get something to eat?" Everyone settled at their table with plates of food and drinks.

After everyone finished their dinner and were chatting, a lady walked over to their table. She was dressed in jeans with orange cowboy boots with an orange cowboy hat that sported a Tennessee sports logo. She looked at Hunt and Karen, "Hey there, I'm sorry to interrupt your dinner, but we all thought we recognized you." She nodded to Riley and Hunt, "I'm with that group of teachers over there." She pointed to the table with a dozen teachers. Three of them were wearing retirement sashes and crowns, "You gentleman took our picture several months ago at the Mexican restaurant in Fairhope. Our friend had just retired after thirty years of teaching and we were celebrating that night."

Riley and Hunt nodded their heads and grinned. "We had such a good time with the congo line that night, we thought we'd invite you youngins' to come line dance with us all. We have requested this in honor of our friends' retirements." The retired teacher looked at everyone at the table and invited the "older youngins" like herself to join in as well, "If you all are interested, we'll see you out there." She tipped her Tennessee orange cowboy hat and made her way back to her friends. Karen looked at the teacher table to see them all waving. They must really have a great time together.

A fiddle began playing and the line dance began. Everyone at the table looked at each other, shrugged and proceeded to join in the line dance. The teacher group was a lot of fun as they moved together like old friends do, moving in and out of the line with Riley, Hunt, Drew, and Curtis. Then the announcer called all of the ladies in the room front and center with the men opposite them. The groups all took turns challenging each other on whether the men or women made for the best line dancers. Curtis, Hunt, Riley and Drew gave everyone a run for their money. Everyone clapped when the music stopped. The teachers hugged the guys and one of them placed a Christmas boa around Drew's neck before going back to their table. Riley laughed at the detective's chagrined expression.

The band was taking a break, so a music selection was played on the intercom in the meantime. "After the Lovin," an old song from the 70's began playing. As the singer crooned the words, Abby and Owen got up to dance. Janet and Edward joined them. Riley asked Toni to dance. Florence winked at them both. As the others at the table watched, Owen and Abby waltzed beautifully with a couple of surprise dips that had everyone laughing. Janet and Edward moved together as he twirled her around the room. Riley and Toni had their own style of gliding across the floor.

Karen looked at everyone and was content. She had Curtis back in her life. She knew there would be more ups and downs. She loved him. They would persevere. She put a hand on his arm. He turned her way, "Would you care to finish out this song with a dance, Mr. Dalton?"

He took her hand and said, "I thought you'd never ask." They walked to the dance floor and he took her in his arms, "So, are we in for some fancy dancing, Miss Smith?" he asked.

She leaned in and kissed him, "I just thought we'd hold each other and move to the music. That's alright with you?"

He looked at her with love in his eyes and said, "Holding you will always be alright with me." They held each other and moved to the music. The song segued into another slow song. Curtis continued to dance with Karen.

Leslie had been talking a little with Wally and realized she liked what was playing, "Would you like to dance?" She had noticed his wedding ring earlier, "If your wife won't mind. I don't see her here."

Wally glanced at Leslie, "No, she won't mind." He held out his hand and walked with her to the dance floor. Wally took her hand in his and she put her hand on his shoulder. As they moved around the dance floor, Leslie asked how he liked working as a chiropractor.

"Make no bones about it, it's a good career," he looked at her with a slight smile.

"Have you met Hunt yet? You have the same sense of humor."

"Yes, I was there for the Santa and the sleigh joke. I actually thought it was kind of funny." Wally looked at Leslie, "What do you do for a living?" She told him about her interior design business. He continued, "I understand from my dad that your mom got that same degree, right?"

Leslie glanced at her mom watching her from their table, "Yes, she worked for a while, then stopped to take care of all of us and the farm. She helped me get my business off the ground and works with me from time to time."

"My dad really took a shine to your mom back in the day. He knew he didn't have a chance when your mom met your dad. He used to tell me they only had eyes for each other, but that didn't stop your mom from being nice to my dad. He said it drove your dad crazy."

"Yes, they have a marriage made in heaven." Leslie was holding his hand with his wedding band. Wally was a nice-looking man. She wondered where his wife was tonight, "So, do you and your wife live in Baldwin County?" Wally didn't answer her. "Look, I don't mean to pry. I'm just being social by asking questions. I just didn't want her walking in and misunderstanding the situation if she saw us dancing. I just met your family tonight. Some wives might not like their husbands dancing with other women."

"I'm trying not to be rude, Leslie, but do you mind if we don't talk about my wife?"

Leslie was dumbfounded, "I apologize, Wally. I didn't realize it was a sensitive subject."

234

"How could you? You don't even know us." She stopped dancing and was very still.

Wally cursed himself for the life he couldn't leave behind and said, "I'm sorry. Thank you for the dance. If you'll excuse me." She wondered what pain he was living with. She couldn't put her finger on it, but she hoped it worked out for him. Leslie watched him walk to the table and say goodnight. He said something to his parents and began to walk out of the room. Before he walked out the door, he turned, and his eyes met hers. She saw sadness and despair reflected there. He nodded to her and then was gone.

As everyone danced, no one noticed Marlena walk out of the building. Tears were falling down her face as she drove home. She couldn't fault Curtis or his girlfriend. She had liked her Moxy for standing up to her. Curtis had picked a good woman, who unless she missed her guess, would be his wife one day. She watched them on the dance floor. They were in love with each other. Marlena cried even harder. She could have had it all. She had missed her chance. She parked on the street in front of her apartment. She spotted Clarence getting out of his car. She was not in the mood for this tonight. She got out of the car and met him on the sidewalk, which was deserted this time of night.

"So, Marlena, Curtis Dalton is not with you. What happened to our agreement?"

She was tired, "Well, Clarence, it looks like you're not going to get what you want after all. How does that feel for once?"

He looked around to make sure no one was on the streets or in their windows watching. Clarence slapped Marlena across the cheek. He grabbed her by the arm and walked towards her apartment," Marlena, who says I'm not going to get what I want? You'll do nicely tonight. Then I'll work on plan B."

Chapter 24

The hoedown was a success, and a lot of money was raised for charity. Everyone stayed behind to help Riley clean the building. It was after midnight when they all left in groups, waving goodnight, and talking about what a good time everyone had.

Curtis was driving Karen home. She had her head on his shoulder and he asked, "How about we drive to the pavilion and I build us a fire? I'm not ready for the evening to end just yet."

Karen raised her head. Her eyes were filled with love for him. He kissed the top of her head and she said, "Let me text Mom to let her know where I'll be and not to wait up. Oh, I don't have a key."

"I've got an extra. Tell her I can let you in." She smiled at Curtis. His heart was full.

"Okay, Mom said not to be too late and for you to be on your best behavior." She laughed and he winked at her.

He pulled up to the pavilion. As she found blankets in the outdoor cabinet, he started the fire. Karen found a

CD player and picked out a CD. As the sultry sounds of jazz resonated in the pavilion, he walked to her, "May I have this dance, Miss Smith?"

She held out her hand, "You may, Mr. Dalton." Curtis drew her into his arms. They held each other and moved around the pavilion. Karen slowly moved her arms up his chest and kissed him. He put his hands on the back of her head and she felt alive. She rubbed her hands down his back, "Curtis, you feel so good."

"Oh, Karen," he took her face in his hands and kissed her deeply. His mouth roamed down her neck. He noticed her top two buttons of her shirt had come undone. He raised his head and looked at the woman he had fallen in love with. Her eyes were filled with longing for him. She unbuttoned her shirt and pulled it open. He put his mouth on hers as his fingers touched her neck. Curtis took a deep breath and whispered her name, "Karen." His eyes met hers. Her gaze revealed love and trust for him. His lips returned to hers as he buttoned her shirt.

Karen raised her head as she saw the desire in his eyes as she felt the solidness of his body. She was so overjoyed for the tenderness he had shown her. She fell deeper in love with him and could no longer keep her silence. She touched his face and said, "I love you."

All the joy that he thought he'd never have burst open in his heart and was mirrored in his eyes as he said, "I love you too."

Exalted by hearing those words, she kissed him deeply. As her mouth left his, she asked, "Can we sit and watch the fire before you have to take me home?"

"Yes, my love. I need to get something first." Curtis walked to his truck and took something out of a cooler. He came back with a bottle of champagne and two glasses, "Courtesy of Riley." Curtis pulled a rocking chair closer to the fire and sat down. She poured two glasses of champagne and handed one to him. She sat on his lap and leaned her head back. They watched the fire and enjoyed the champagne. Teardrops began to trickle down her face because of her feelings for this man, "I love you so much Curtis."

He kissed the top of her head as he told her how he felt about her, "I love you too, Karen." They held each other. For the next few moments, this time was theirs.

Love from Farm to Stable

Chapter 25

After Curtis drove Karen home, he worked his way back to his house. He parked in the driveway and looked at his watch. It was 2 AM. He hadn't been out this late in a long time. Of course, he hadn't had the fortune of being with Karen like this before. He sat in his truck and thought about the night. They loved each other. He truly was a lucky guy. He started to get out of his truck when he heard his phone ring. Maybe it was Karen telling him she loved him one more time before they went to sleep. He smiled, but then frowned when he saw it was his dad's number, "Dad, everything okay? Marlena? Now, Dad... What? When? Yes, I'll come pick you and Mom up and we'll go to the hospital. Okay, I'll be right there."

Curtis dropped the phone on the seat. He couldn't believe it. He made a call to Edward and explained everything. Edward agreed they'd all stay inside today, and he'd wake Karen and get her to call Candace. Curtis called Riley and asked him to be careful today and to explain things to Florence, Hunt and Toni. Curtis backed up and drove down the road to his sister's house, calling her before his truck landed in her driveway. His headlights shone on her locking her door. She got in the truck and they picked up their parents.

As they made their way to the hospital, their dad filled them in on what happened, "Apparently, Marlena had an alliance with Clarence Higgins III. Marlena's dad had been diagnosed with leukemia. Insurance hadn't covered everything. Marshall, Marlena's dad, had been too proud to ask anyone for the money. He sold some of his land. She told her dad insurance finally came through, even though it was Clarence providing the money for Marshall's treatments. He didn't know this until tonight and he's heartbroken. He felt he drove his daughter to this. Marshall said he would have figured it out if she had only come to him. She felt she had no choice. She knew Clarence from her mom's country club back when they were still members. Owen looked at his son, "She wanted to make amends with us. That's why Marshall called. She was beaten pretty badly."

Curtis glanced at his dad's face in the rearview mirror. It was filled with anger. Curtis responded, "I called everyone and put them on alert. Detective Myers is meeting us at the hospital." They made it to the hospital in record time. Hunt had just started his shift. He met them at the door and walked them up to Marlena's room. He told them about her prognosis: broken ribs and lacerations. He kept the worst part to himself; she had been raped. Hunt told the family that with a little time, she would be well physically. But it would take much longer for her mind to heal. He left them to go on his rounds.

The family came into the room and saw her dad sitting by her bedside with tears in his eyes. Owen came to his chair and hugged him, "Marshall."

Marshall hugged him back, "I never should have let it come to this. I didn't know she would do this. Her mom had to take a walk down the hallway because as her mother, she blames herself. Marlena woke at one point and just talked to me. I think she needed to get it all out of her system." Marshall looked at Abby and Curtis, "She wanted me to tell you she was so sorry for not helping your family in your time of need. Curtis, she especially wanted to talk to you. She wanted to apologize." Marshall had tears in his eyes.

There was movement from the hospital bed. Marlena was awake and looking at her dad, "Dad?" She turned towards her father and her face showed the marks of where Clarence had beaten her. One eye had been blackened. Marshall touched her hand. Marlena looked at the Daltons, "Curtis, it's so good to see you. Mrs. Dalton, I'm so sorry."

Tears fell from Abby's eyes as she approached the hospital bed. She put her hand on Marlena's, "I am so sorry for what has happened to you. I'm fine. You don't need to worry about me. Sometimes, life has a way of showing you what's important. We're going to help you heal. You're a good girl."

Marlena started to shake her head and cry, "No ma'am, I don't deserve to live with how I've treated people. I'm a horrible human being." Marlena met Curtis's gaze. He had tears in his eyes, "Curtis, can you move closer?" He walked to the bed and put her hand in his, "I'm so sorry about tonight. I didn't want to do any of that. That was Clarence's plan. He said he'd tell my father everything if I wouldn't help him get to you. I knew Dad would be disappointed in me. But part of me wanted to be close to you one more time. We had a good thing. I just wanted to be surrounded by your integrity. You are such a wonderful man."

She was having trouble breathing, so he replied, "Marlena, it's okay. Please rest and save your breath."

She shook her head as the tears fell down her face and she grabbed his hand, "It's not okay. I could have been your wife. But I was stupid. I let it all fall apart." She was breathing heavily, "Curtis, water please." He picked up the water cup and she sipped water through a straw. "Thank you." She continued to hold his hand, "Your girlfriend. Karen, is it?" He nodded his head. "You love each other, don't you?"

He replied, "Yes, Marlena, we love each other."

"I could tell. You never looked at me like that." He started to speak. "No, you know I'm telling the truth. You look at her like you can't breathe without her. That's special. I hope you both know how special that is." She started to cough, and he held her water cup for her. She touched his hand, "Be good to each other, okay? Even if

244

you have disagreements, please work them out. You two look good together. She's a sweet girl, isn't she?" He nodded. "I could tell. She has a lightness about her, but a toughness too. It took guts to cut me off at the pass. I thought then that she must truly love you to fight for you." She coughed and took a deep breath, "Be happy, Curtis."

She let go of his hand. He leaned down and kissed her forehead, "There's no forgiveness necessary, Marlena. It was just not our time."

She nodded and turned to her dad, who was crying, "Dad, I'm so sorry. I couldn't lose you. I love you, Dad." Marlena grimaced and touched her ribs. Her toughness emerged as she breathed heavily to say the words, "Bastard broke my ribs." She looked at the Daltons, "I need to speak to the police. I know Clarence's dad will cover this up." She coughed. Leslie walked over to give her more water. Marlena held a hand up, "I need to get this out. I clawed down his face with my nails. He was in such a rage; he didn't even think to clean under my nails."

Owen said, "I'll get the detective. I believe he's here." He walked out the door.

Abby came to stand by Marlena, "You're a brave girl and I meant what I said before. You are a good girl. You made a mistake, but you are strong enough to overcome this. You have a purpose to see justice. If you have a purpose in life, you can do anything you want, if you use what you have to help others. I believe in you."

Marlena pointed to the water cup. Abby helped her take a sip. Marlena touched her hand, "Mrs. D, I am so glad you beat the cancer. You're a wonderful mom and a nice lady."

"I haven't heard someone call me Mrs. D in a long time. It's nice to hear that name again."

Abby's tears flowed. Leslie stepped forward, "We'll all help you."

Marlena looked at Leslie. "It would have been nice to have you for a sister." She blew out a breath. Her ribs were killing her. She looked at Curtis then back at Leslie, "I never believed him when he said you were a brat." Part of Marlena's mouth curved, and she winced.

He smiled as his sister turned to him, "Well, he's always been a pain in the …"

Her mom interrupted her, "Leslie Dalton, we are in a hospital. Have some manners."

Marshall smiled through his tears, "It's nice to be a parent to these young people. Even when they do things that aren't always right, we still love them." He touched his daughter's cheek and the tears flowed even more when he gazed at her bruises, "Dads are supposed to protect their daughters. I'm so sorry I failed you."

Marlena put her hand in his, "Dad, I love you." She coughed and took a breath, "I'm so tired." She turned her face to rest on her pillow, "I'm just so tired." She drifted off to sleep.

Marshall told the Daltons the nurses had given her something to sleep. He was glad she was finally able to rest, "Thank you all for coming and helping my daughter to start healing. I appreciate what everyone said."

Owen entered the room holding Edwina, Marlena's mom. Detective Myers was right behind them. Abby walked over to them, "She's just fallen asleep." Abby hugged Edwina, who was crying. Detective Myers pulled out a pair of gloves and a plastic bag. While Marlena slept, he collected evidence he hoped would put away a true villain for the rest of his life.

Clarence Higgins III was in a rage. He barely made it home with the storm building inside him. He gazed in the mirror at the scratches down his face, "Damn bitch. Should have killed her." He left her alive in the hope that somehow, she'd contact Curtis Dalton. He knew the Daltons would go see Marlena. Because that's what that sappy family did. It was all love and sunshine with them. It made them sick to his stomach.

But, if he could get Karen alone while they were away, it will have been worth it.

Love from Farm to Stable

Chapter 26

It was after 4 AM by the time the family got back to the farm. They left Marshall their numbers and told him to call anytime. The family members would be happy to take turns sitting with his daughter. Everyone had been quiet on the way home, deep in their own thoughts. Curtis had dropped his parents off first and made sure they got into their house safely. Next, he dropped off his sister. She gave him a hug. He made sure she got into her house and locked the door. He couldn't face going to sleep yet. He heard his phone buzz and he pulled over to read his screen.

A text had popped up from Karen, *"I'm still awake if you want to talk. I love you."*

"Yes, I would like that. Would your mom and Edward mind?"

"No, they're fine with that. I'll be waiting."

He pulled up to the house to see Karen running out to him. He got out of the truck and met her half-way. He caught her up in his arms and held on. She held him tight. He took her face in his hands and kissed her, "I love you."

She kissed him back and asked, "How is she?"

He rubbed his hands down his face, "Are you sure you want me to tell you? "

"Yes, please. I need to know."

He took a breath, "That bastard beat her badly. She has broken ribs and bruises all over her face." Curtis wearily eyed the swing on the front porch, "Can we sit, please?" She put her arm around him and led him to the swing. "She apologized to my family. She told me she was sorry for how she treated me tonight. She didn't mean any of it. She said Clarence pushed her into doing it to get back at us. He was giving her money to pay for her dad's medical bills in exchange for her helping him."

"I'm so sorry," she put her head on his shoulder.

He looked at the woman he loved and said, "You know, she actually said she admired you for standing up for yourself tonight. I always thought her to be self-centered after what happened when Mom had cancer. We were both young when we were in a relationship. The families all talked, and we forgave her. She's had a rough time of it. Marlena is going to need to talk to someone."

"I really like the therapist I see. Maybe as time passes, I can reach out," she glanced at Curtis, "that is if it wouldn't be too awkward."

He put his arm around her and kissed the top of her head, "I think with time, she'd like that. Thank you for the thought." Someone had left a blanket sitting on the railing of the porch. She pulled it over them both. With the events of the night behind them and the gliding feel of the swing, snuggled together, they promptly fell asleep.

A rooster crowing had Curtis opening his eyes to the dawn of a new day. His head had been propped up by his hand on the arm of the swing. He yawned as he never felt so tired in all his life. He looked over at Karen, who was fast asleep. He pulled her closer to him and rested his chin on top of her head.

He saw the door open. Edward held two cups of coffee, one which he handed to Curtis and he took a sip, "Oh, you're a good man, Edward. I may make it after all." He took another sip of coffee as he watched Edward close the door and lower himself into the rocking chair next to the swing.

Edward rubbed his face, "This reminds me of stakeouts I used to work when I was with the precinct. Around the clock, lots of coffee and little sleep." He gazed at Curtis, "How's Marlena?"

"She's had a rough time of it." He told Edward about the bruises and broken ribs.

"Bastard," Edward managed to say. He sipped his coffee and let the warmness wash away the bitterness he felt towards some people. He hated abusers. Edward saw enough of that when he was on the force to last a lifetime.

"She's a smart girl. She clawed his face, so Detective Myers has some evidence."

"Good for her," Edward said, "maybe that will help put him away. But I'm afraid it's not always that easy." Curtis nodded his head. He sipped more coffee as Karen moved to be closer to him. She continued to sleep. Edward motioned to her, "So, did you two settle things?"

Curtis's mouth curved, "Yes. We had a nice night, or should I say morning, watching the fire I built at the pavilion." He looked at Edward, "I love her."

"Did you tell her that?"

"Yes, fortunately she loves me too."

"Life can be a wonder," Edward looked at the woman he thought of as his daughter, "I'm so glad her uncle is dead. Neither one of those girls deserved what happened in their childhood. Janet still beats herself up about it and tells the girls how sorry she is that she wasn't stronger. The girls just hug her and tell her she did the best she could in keeping them all alive and together. They're good girls." Curtis nodded his head in agreement. Edward looked around as Janet came out on the porch bundled up in a sweater holding a cup of coffee. She walked over and rubbed her hand gently over her daughter's hair. She sat next to Edward and sipped her coffee, content in the knowledge that, in this moment, her family was safe and loved.

Karen began to stir. She opened her eyes and saw Ed and her mom sitting on the porch. She sat up and looked at Curtis, "Good morning."

He kissed her on the forehead, "Hi yourself."

"So, did anyone think to bring me coffee?" Curtis held his cup out to her. "Who made that?" She looked at Ed and he nodded, "No way. That's cop coffee. Do you know that's pure sludge you're drinking?"

He chuckled as he pulled his cup back and continued sipping his coffee, "This coffee is so strong, it would put hair on your chest."

She looked at the man she loved and said, "Have you lost your mind? I don't need hair on my chest, thank you." Edward laughed. Karen rolled her eyes and asked, "What does your day look like, Curtis?"

"I might go home and get a little more shut eye. I have some errands to run later if you want to come along." She leaned her head on his shoulder, "I can do that." She put her hand to her mouth as she covered a yawn. She patted his knee and leaned over to kiss him, "I'm going in to get more sleep. I'll set my alarm. What time should I be ready?"

He kissed her back, "How 'bout I take you out to lunch and let's say noon?" She kissed him one more time as she wrapped the blanket around her and headed for the door. She hugged her mom on her way inside.

Karen turned at the door and looked at Curtis. She put her hand over her heart. He did the same and smiled.

Love from Farm to Stable

Chapter 27

It was Monday evening. Everyone was very aware of what happened to Marlena and the police were working on locating Clarence Higgins. So far, no luck. The thought was that his dad was hiding him, but Detective Myers was keeping them up to date. The Dalton Farm was as secure as could be with cameras, security tightened, and all occupants of the farm prepared to protect their families. Curtis and his family felt secure in the knowledge that everyone was on alert. Therefore, he left early Monday morning for a business trip to Montgomery. He would return Tuesday night.

Karen had worked at the coffee shop all day Monday. She couldn't believe she had her master's degree. She was ready to work on the next step in getting a job in the hospital setting. Her thoughts turned to Curtis. They had spent most of Sunday together and the families had gathered for dinner at the Big House last night. He had lingered with her on the swing before they had to go into their respective homes for the night. She kissed him good night and wished him a safe trip. He returned her kiss and winked at her before driving home. That night she texted him a picture of them Leslie had taken at the hoedown.

"Just a reminder of how glad I am that we found each other. I love you, Curtis. Please be safe on the road. See you tomorrow night."

"Karen, I'm glad we found each other too. These road trips will be easier now knowing I have you to come home to. My life is not lonely anymore. I love you with all my heart. Sleep well, all my love. Curtis."

Karen was so glad family and friends had seen past what some may consider an age barrier in their relationship. Once they saw the couple were confident in their love, that removed any doubts. Candace had walked Karen out to her car after work. There had been no sign of anything unusual there. Florence had called and with a recommendation from Detective Myers, would be picking up her sister and their mom for a night out. The detective had recommended one of the safest restaurants, he thought, because it was next door to the police precinct. Florence had driven them to the restaurant he had recommended. It was a Mexican restaurant called Cobalt Blue. When the ladies entered the restaurant, the smells of sizzling meat and vegetables fueled their hunger. Seated next to a roaring fire, a round of margaritas was ordered. Chips and salsa immediately were placed on the table. As they munched on chips and drank margaritas, the ladies chatted.

Florence couldn't wait for what she considered her second honeymoon after Christmas. She and Riley were still making plans but hadn't really settled on a place. Their thoughts had travelled from Destin to New Orleans to the Smoky Mountains. Karen thought all her sister's options sounded romantic. Janet talked about how busy it was at the office and she was looking forward to a Christmas bonus. Their mom reminded them that Christmas was only a short time away and told the girls to look for a nice Christmas present in their stockings this year. The girls smiled and knew how hard their mom worked. Florence asked Karen about Curtis. Karen's smile reached her eyes, "He's good. Traveling to Montgomery on business and will be back tomorrow night." Karen took a sip of her drink. Janet talked about Christmas with the Daltons. Karen and Florence agreed to bring some side dishes. Florence was excited that Aunt Alice and Mary would be joining them. She told them Hunt was going to be with his parents for Christmas. It should be a nice holiday. The ladies held up their glasses and clinked them together for good luck.

Clarence Higgins III was waiting down the street from Cobalt Blue. He thought about his last night with Marlena. He began to get aroused. He was going to have a damn scar from those scratches. If the cops ever caught up with him, they couldn't prove a thing. He'd had sex with Marlena and nothing more. He knew she liked the sex. She had just been playing hard to get. Just like Karen

Smith. He laughed. Karen thought she would be safe in a restaurant next to a police station. She was so naive.

He was in a nondescript car with an UBER sticker on it that no one would question and so far, it was working. No one had paid the least bit of attention to him. Clarence glanced at his Rolex. An hour had passed, and he just needed to be patient. His plan came to mind with kidnapping Karen. He was flush with cash and had a cabin all set aside in the woods they'd never find. The knockout drug he had gotten from a supplier was all he needed to make sure she wouldn't get away this time. Clarence glanced out his front windshield and waited. Those women she was with wouldn't stand a chance, especially when he held a pistol to Karen's head. Half an hour later, he spotted them exiting the restaurant door and eased his hands on the steering wheel. The car was put into drive and it slowly moved forward. Clarence braked, "What the hell?" His eyes widened in disbelief. There was that damn detective. Myers, that was his name.

Two cops were hanging with him. Damn! He couldn't very well shoot cops at point blank range. His dad wasn't that good and wouldn't be able to get him out of that one. Clarence watched the two sisters and the mother drive off from the restaurant. He could follow them, but he had a better plan in mind. Clarence pulled out and decided to drive back home. He thought out loud, "I tried the coffee shop, I tried the beach, I tried this restaurant." Clarence sighed, but then grinned and thought about the Dalton farm. His dad told him to leave them alone. He imitated his dad's whiny voice, "The Daltons have powerful contacts in the political and local community not to mention Washington, DC. Leave them alone." The old man was not useful anymore. That was possibly a loose end he needed to tie up. He chortled, "I'm going to take it to the farm. Bunch of damn rednecks and cowboys playing dress up, that's the Daltons. They just happened to have money, but they can't begin to mess with Clarence."

Research and a few buddies that had kept tabs on the Daltons had Clarence outfitted with all kinds of information. There was a sister who lived on the property as well. A hellish grin covered his face. Maybe he could have double the fun. It would be priceless as he learned this one was friends with the pretty blonde, he'd had some fun with at that pizza place years ago. He would pay her a visit, then go after the real prize, Karen Smith. Clarence pulled in his driveway and turned the car off. He just had to get Curtis Dalton out of the way first. The cell phone sitting on the car seat buzzed. His face widened into a grin as he answered the phone, "Well, speak of the devil. Yes, you have tabs on our friend? Good, good." Clarence cackled, "Yes, I don't think he'll be making it home to the farm tomorrow night. Anything can happen on the interstate. Tires blow out all the time. Uh-huh. You get the job done and we'll settle up afterwards. Yep. That's the way it works." He chuckled as the buddy helping him would be taken care of in more ways than one. Right after

Curtis Dalton was history. Clarence Higgins III whistled as he walked into his house.

Chapter 28

Curtis left Montgomery behind about an hour ago. Stopping at a gas station before he left meant a full tank of gas and caffeine for the road. Sipping a cup of coffee and listening to a local country station, he was cruising towards home. He had talked business with his parents last night. He called Karen right before he left earlier tonight. The happiness and the excitement in her voice because he was coming home played over and over in his head. Curtis never thought he would find a soulmate, but he had found one in her. Dusk had fallen a few hours ago. Darkness surrounded the interstate. The road was deserted except for a handful of cars. The holiday traffic wouldn't begin in earnest for a couple more weeks. He was ready to be home.

A red truck was slowing down in front of him, and he assumed it was heading for the exit ahead. Curtis put on his blinker, merged over to the left lane, passed the truck and cruised back into the right lane. Bright lights switched on behind him and were advancing on his truck. No other cars were around him at this time and the only one he had passed was the red truck, which he thought had turned off the interstate. He rolled his window down and signaled for the car to go around him. The car sped up and maintained speed right next to his truck. Curtis glanced to his left, saw a gun point out of the window and shoot his left front tire. The red truck took off in a hurry as he tried to hold the steering wheel in a firm grip, but the loss of traction had the truck careening off the interstate into the woods. He tried to slow down and not hit the brakes, but the truck had a mind of its own, bouncing through the woods until it was stopped by a tree. The airbags deployed. There was nothing to be heard but silence.

Abby and Owen Dalton were playing cards at their kitchen table on Tuesday night. Christmas would be here soon, and the couple had finished mapping out their plans for a day with friends and family. Abby took a sip of wine as she watched her husband throw down a royal flush. She rolled her eyes, "Owen Dalton, that is the third time you've won. I think you're cheating."

With a twinkle in his eyes, Owen took a sip of his beer, "Abby, my love, I won fair and square." As his cell phone buzzed on the counter, he got up and walked towards his phone. He kissed his wife on the top of her head, "I can't wait to collect my winnings tonight from you." He looked back at his wife as he answered the phone. She grinned at her husband and shuffled the cards for the next round.

"Hello? Yes, this is Owen Dalton. Curtis Dalton? Yes, he's my son." Abby glanced up at Owen and he met her gaze. His face paled. His wife came around the table to stand by him and put her hand on his arm, "Yes, we'll be right there. Thank you."

"Owen, what happened?"

Tears were in his eyes, "It's Curtis. He ran off the road outside of Montgomery. He was life flighted to the trauma hospital in Mobile." Abby was pulling on her coat and handed a jacket to her husband. He grabbed his keys, and they worked their way to the truck. Owen backed out of the driveway. His wife reached for the phone to call their daughter. It went to voicemail. She looked at her husband with tears in her eyes. She tried Leslie again, "I can't reach her." The truck had reached the end of the farm road as Owen turned onto the highway towards Mobile.

"Try her again." He reached over for his wife's hand as tears flowed down his face.

"Owen, we can't lose another son. I can't go through this again." He squeezed her hand and she asked, "What else did they tell you?"

"That was a deputy that called. Apparently, he had turned onto the interstate and happened to see Curtis's truck go off the road. Thank God, because it went into the woods, and I don't want to think what would have happened if no one had seen it." He wiped his face and cleared his throat, "The deputy said it looked like a tire blew, which caused the truck to go out of control into the woods." He glanced at her, "Honey, he crashed into a tree."

She sobbed, "Owen, he's alive, right? They would have told you otherwise. Please, Owen."

He continued to squeeze her hand and talked through his tears, "The airbag cushioned the blow to his head, but Curtis has a concussion, broken ribs and possibly a broken arm. He's alive. We need to keep thinking good thoughts. He's tough and has a lot to live for."

Abby squeezed his hand, "Karen! She'll be waiting for him. He was supposed to meet her when he got home." She fumbled for her phone and dialed a number as tears rolled down her cheeks, "Florence, this is Abby. Listen, I need your help."

Chapter 29

Leslie Dalton had chosen Tuesday night to walk the streets of downtown Fairhope. She loved the solitude as she soaked in all the window displays that various merchants had assembled for the holidays. She loved her job as an interior designer. Leslie had been on the phone all day and finally had turned it off, needing a break. She had her hands in her coat pocket due to the chill in the air. As she reached her destination, Leslie entered the small building at the corner of the block. Their specialty was fish tacos and was her favorite. She'd get an order to go and drive down to the pier to eat while taking in the view of the bay.

"Hello, Leslie."

She turned around and standing behind her was Wally Sternum, Jr. Leslie hadn't seen him since that night at the Christmas Country Hoedown when he left her standing on the dance floor. They had been dancing when Leslie asked about his wife joining him that night. He was obviously married due to the wedding ring on his hand. Apparently, she didn't know why, but he didn't want her asking questions about his wife and left the dance. Being the social creature that she was Leslie nodded her head, "Hello, Wally. What brings you to town on a Tuesday night?" With his dark hair, blue eyes and what looked like a year 'round tan, Leslie had no trouble conversing with him. That is, if he would only talk to her.

He glanced at Leslie, who had intrigued him the first time he met her at the dance. He tried to interact by dancing with her. It had ended poorly when he had shut her down when she asked about his wife. He ended up being rude to her and leaving that night, "This happens to be my favorite place downtown. I like their fish tacos."

Her eyes widened in agreement, "Well, good job Wally Sternum. Those happen to be my favorite as well."

He smiled inwardly at the sparkle in her eyes. With her long blondish brunette hair and her brown eyes, she was a beauty. In the short time they had talked at the dance, he felt she took no prisoners, but had a kindness about her as well. He got the impression she was a fixer, but she wouldn't be able to fix him. He was beyond repair.

"Next please," said the cashier.

"Excuse me, Wally." Leslie put in her order, then Wally was next with his. As they waited for their food, she turned to him, "Where are you headed from here?"

He offered, "I just thought I'd sit at one of the tables out back to eat and then head home."

Leslie eyed Wally and made a decision, "How 'bout we follow each other down to the pier and eat together? The view is a lot nicer down there."

Wally put his hands in his pocket and thought about his choices. He could eat alone or be in the company of a beautiful woman for the next hour, "Sure, that sounds good." Their orders were delivered into their hands and they made their way to the pier.

Once settled at one of the many picnic tables by the parking lot, they unwrapped their tacos. Once she had taken a few bites, she gazed out at the darkness of the night which was a beautiful backdrop for all the lights that lit up the pier and the bay. The martin houses extending from the bottom of the bay towards the sky added contrast to the beauty. Leslie sighed, "It just doesn't get any better than this."

"Sure, it does," said Wally in between bites of his own taco. He sipped from his bottle of water and swallowed, "Nights on the water in Key West will knock your socks off."

"Really Wally Sternum? When did you go to Key West?" She was fascinated to find out he had a few layers that piqued her interest.

"I actually went down there during a biology field trip in high school. It was a pretty cool trip. The scenery was beautiful." He glanced at Leslie.

Her eyes held humor, "Were high school girls in bikinis part of that scenery?"

He wiped his mouth with a napkin. Laughter lit up his eyes and a grin formed on his face," Maybe."

Wow, she thought. Talk about knocking your socks off. Sure, he was good-looking, but that grin turned his

267

face into pure sexy. Leslie bit into her taco and a bit of sauce landed on her lips. She licked the sauce with her tongue and Wally was entranced. He took a sip of water and looked out over the bay to get his mind off her lips. "How is your dad, Wally? It was nice to meet your parents at the hoedown. Your mom seems sweet."

"Yeah, they're great. Mom can be sweet until you cross her. She's no one's fool, that's for sure. Dad? Well, Dad's a rock." This was the most Leslie bet he ever talked about his life and she was delighted. Wally didn't know how much he wanted to say about his parents, but she was easy to talk to, so he continued, "I went through a rough time, and they were both there to help me through it. I went into business with my dad. We have a good relationship there too, so it's worked out well, so far." He took a sip of his water.

Leslie's attention was hooked, "You're both chiropractors, right?"

He remembered their conversation at the hoedown that didn't end well. He was rude to her and had no business treating her that way. She didn't know his story. His parents had raised him better than that. Wally took a deep breath and gazed into her beautiful brown eyes, "Listen. I want to apologize to you. I shouldn't have been rude to you at the dance that night. I don't usually talk about my private life to anyone but my parents and even then, I don't like to say much."

Leslie was stunned with his apology for being rude at the dance. She really didn't know what to say to him, so she did what came naturally to her. She put her hand on his, "Wally, you were right that night. I don't know your family or your situation. It was rude of me to ask."

He turned his hand over until he was holding hers, "How about we agree to disagree? I do need to explain. I want to explain, so you'll understand." He cleared his throat, "My wife died a long time ago and I still miss her. I always felt I could have done more to save her life. I have yet to meet another woman that I want to try to have a life with, so I'll continue to wear my wedding ring until I do."

Leslie hung on to his hand, "I'm so sorry, Wally, I didn't understand, but I'm glad you talked to me about her." She patted his hand and let it go, "You know, we lost our brother when he was killed by a drunk driver a few years ago. It brought Curtis and me closer together. Of course, he can be a real pain, but what am I going to do, he's my brother, right?"

Leslie's eyes held a smile that matched the ones on her lips. He hadn't really noticed before tonight what beautiful eyes she had and how they made her face even more radiant when she smiled. He wouldn't mind talking with her a little while longer as another night of loneliness stretched out before him. Wally decided to ask, "Leslie, do you have anywhere to be? Would you have time to take a walk with me on the pier?" He held his breath as he was no good at this. He was out of practice.

"I would love to take a walk on the pier." After clearing their table, they walked underneath the pier entrance sign and began talking about their families as they strolled. Leslie reminded him that if things had gone differently with his dad and her mom, they wouldn't be here talking now. His mouth tilted up and her heart skipped a beat. As they passed the pier restaurant that had been a mainstay for years, Wally told Leslie about his parents having their after-wedding rehearsal dinner there. She told him about the time she had a date with a guy who owned one of the boats docked at this marina connected to the pier restaurant. They stopped there and stood by the railing to the marina. There were a few big sailboats moored there tonight.

She laughed and said, "It was not a good afternoon for my date."

Wally enjoyed hearing her laughter, "What happened?"

"We left the marina and went out on the bay. My date was cute and all, so I didn't mind when he leaned over to kiss me." Wally raised an eyebrow. "I felt queasy about fifteen minutes into the ride and the boat suddenly shifted." She glanced at Wally, "I threw up all over his shoes." He grimaced. She shook her head at the memory, "Yeah, he never asked me out again."

"Did you at least help him clean up his boat?"

Her eyes twinkled, "Yeah, and he told me that was okay, he'd just hose it down." Wally had a serious look on his face as he imagined the cleanup.

"Come on Sternum, lighten up. You wouldn't see any humor in that situation if it happened to you?" Wally was charmed by her sense of fun and positive outlook.

"Well, that depends." Leslie noticed him gaze at her mouth.

She took a breath and asked him, "Depends on what?"

He moved closer, "It depends on when I lean over to kiss you, if you'll be throwing up on my shoes."

She leaned closer to him, "Well, you are kind of cute and we aren't on a boat. How 'bout you take a chance?"

Wally met her halfway as she put her lips on his. They let the kiss happen. It was extraordinary thought Leslie. He put his arms around her and deepened the kiss. He touched her hair as he kissed her. He hadn't felt this way since…He broke off the kiss and quickly stepped back.

"Wally?" Leslie touched his arm as the desire she observed on his face a minute ago had disappeared, like a switch had been turned off. His face was void of any emotion. Leslie wanted to comfort him, "It's okay, Wally. I understand."

He saw the kindness in her eyes. She was perfect, but she wasn't his to have, "I'm sorry. I think it's time I walked you back to your car."

"Okay, "she answered. He held the door open for her. Before Leslie got in her car, she touched his arm, "I'm not sure what I can do to help, but I hope you find peace." She handed him a business card, "That's my cell and work number. Please call me anytime if you want to talk." She leaned over and kissed his cheek, "Thank you for tonight.

I enjoyed myself. Bye." He closed her door and walked to his car. She watched him drive away. She would do her best to help him heal. Leslie looked at the bright moon shining over Mobile Bay, which illuminated the tranquility of the water. She sighed at its beauty. Leslie rummaged in her purse and looked at her phone, "Oh, no. Shoot. Mom called." She saw several missed calls from her mother. Her pulse began to race. She dialed her number, "Mom, what's wrong? Curtis? Oh my God. I'm on my way."

Leslie made it to the trauma hospital in record time. She spotted her mom and dad talking to a doctor and joined in by listening to the conversation. She put her arm around her mother and Abby held on to her daughter. She understood that her brother had a concussion, two broken ribs and a sprained arm. Her dad told her it was better than what they believed his injuries to be when the deputy had called earlier. The doctor left the three of them alone. Leslie was in tears and her dad pulled her into his arms, "Honey, he's tough. You know that."

She looked up at him, "He's alive, right Dad? He's going to live? I can't lose another brother, Dad. I just can't." Owen held her as she cried. Leslie felt a hand on her back and turned around. Karen was there to comfort her. She turned to hug Karen as she saw the devastated look on her face, "Oh, we're a mess. We can't let Curtis see us like this." Leslie swiped at her mascara, "He'd call me something like raccoon eyes or bat face." She laughed through her tears and Karen's mouth curved before she burst into tears. Leslie held her.

Florence walked up to put an arm around Abby to give comfort and remarked, "He's going to be okay. Curtis is like a brother to me, and I can't lose him."

As tears fell down her face, she held Abby and asked if she and Owen had been in to see him. "Not yet. We're waiting for them to move him to ICU, then we can see him." Abby focused on everyone here for Curtis. Janet and Edward had traveled with Florence, Riley and Karen. The families had become close to each other and she really liked that. Owen suggested everyone sit together while they waited to see Curtis. Edward and Riley rounded up coffee for the group. A nurse brought them a box of Kleenex. As eyes were wiped and coffee sipped, Leslie observed a man stopping at the front desk and got up to meet him.

"Henry!" Leslie's best friend and assistant in her design business pulled her in for a big hug.

"Honey, I'm glad you texted me. How is Curtis?" She had tears rolling down her face. Henry gave her his handkerchief, "Now, honey, dry your eyes. You know when you go to see him, he's going to call you bat girl or raccoon face. Now, you don't want to give him that satisfaction, do you? Hmm?"

Leslie laughed through her tears, "Right, Henry? We both know him so well." She hugged him again. They walked arm in arm to sit with the families. Henry hugged her parents and was introduced to everyone else.

An hour later, the doctor came back to see the group with Hunt. Curtis had been moved to ICU and would be ready for the family to come back two at a time shortly. The doctor said the prognosis looked good. His arm was sprained, not broken. The concussion was being monitored and the ribs would take a little time to heal. Curtis would need rest. He could probably be released in a couple of days. Owen and Abby thanked the doctor and hugged each other. Everyone in the group felt a little lighter. Hunt said a few words of encouragement to Curtis's parents and then he came over to hug Karen, "Hey Hon, he's going to be good as new, okay?" She nodded her head and wiped her tears and he said, "You two have a lot to look forward to in your life. Just think, when he's recovering at home, you can finish reading him Pride and Prejudice. He'd really like that, huh?" Hunt rolled his eyes.

Karen laughed through her tears, "I see you heard about that." She stared at Florence, who shrugged and smiled. Hunt sat down with Karen, Riley and Florence to wait. Riley asked Hunt if he was on call here too. He told him he was on a sub list here but had finished his time for tonight when he saw Curtis come in, so he stuck around to check on him. Karen put her hand on his and held it. He squeezed her hand.

The doctor came out to take Abby and Owen to see Curtis. Karen got up because she just couldn't sit anymore. She headed towards the window to look out at the night and hugged herself while waiting to see Curtis. Thoughts of him swirled through her head and she smiled. His sense of humor. The first time he kissed her after taking her to the movies. Holding her after she was sick and had a nightmare. Sitting up with her in the rocking chair in her bedroom. Waking up to him holding her on the front porch after Marlena had been beaten by Clarence Higgins. She took a deep breath. He was still out there. She observed the two families who were looking out for each other. They had become close, and Karen was grateful.

Karen felt a hand on her arm. "Hey, Hon," Owen had come to let her know she could go back with Leslie to see Curtis, "He's not pretty, but he's going to be 100% once he recovers." Owen smiled at her. She hugged him. "That's my girl. He's going to be fine."

Leslie and Karen made their way back to see Curtis. He turned to look at them. Leslie reached over and touched his arm, "Well, you really did it this time. Such a jerk for making me cry. What else is new?"

Curtis moved his hand to touch hers. He breathed out, "Batgirl?"

"Ugh. You're such an ass, Curtis." Leslie leaned down and kissed him on the head, "But, at least your ours." She turned towards Karen, "Here, maybe Karen can hear something nice come out of your mouth, huh?" She stepped up to the bedrail. Tears were running down her face.

"Hey, love," Curtis took a small breath, "Going to be okay." She held his hand and nodded. "Glad you're safe. Don't go alone. Nowhere alone." She looked back at Leslie, who had a question in her eyes.

Karen leaned over and kissed him lightly on the mouth, "I love you. The families are here. We're all safe."

He touched her hand and looked at her face, "Promise me. Stay with family. Promise me."

"I promise Curtis." His eyes closed and he drifted off to sleep. The nurse came over to let them know it was time to go. Karen touched his hand one more time and walked out with Leslie. They were deep in thought as they joined the families.

Detective Myers turned towards Karen, "Miss Smith, may I have a word with you?"

Everyone was looking at her. "What's going on?"

Florence joined Karen, "Come on Hon, let's talk to Drew."

They walked over to an isolated part of the lobby. Detective Myers began, "Miss Smith, Deputy Lewis called me. After investigating the truck, it seems a bullet was found in Mr. Dalton's tire. We think this is what caused the tire to blow sending his car into that tree. We don't feel this is random and believe that Clarence is putting another plan in action. He is dangerous. Our police psychologist feels he has lost all sense of reality and is obsessed with getting to you, Miss Smith."

Karen gazed at the detective and motioned for Leslie to join them, "Curtis knew something was wrong." His sister faced Karen, who said, "Leslie and I both just heard Curtis ask if I was safe and told me not to be alone."

Leslie nodded, "Curtis told Karen to stay with family and go nowhere alone." The detective looked around the lobby and gazed at Karen.

"Miss Smith, you should take his advice. Stay with family." They walked back over to the group as Drew addressed them all, "Folks, I would like you all to stay in groups as much as possible. If you live alone, stay with a family member." Owen looked at Leslie and said they would make sure she and her dog would stay with them. Drew continued, "Remember your signal to text on your cell phones if you get in trouble and have time to put that message in. If that fails, remember you are all connected with signals to each other to find the person's location." Drew glanced at Owen, "Mr. Dalton, I'm sending a couple of cars to patrol your property. I also have stationed a guard at your son's door here."

Owen gave the detective his thanks. Abby stood by her husband as he put his arm around her. Abby told Owen she was checking in with the nurse's station before they left. Everyone then exited the building, escorted by Detective Myers. Karen thought about Curtis on the way home. Tears ran down her face. He was hurt because of her. This needed to stop now. She was going to follow the detective's plan, but she had an idea. One that would end all their suffering.

Love from Farm to Stable

Chapter 30

Friday morning, Curtis woke up in his parents' home. He was released from the hospital Thursday afternoon. His ribs were sore, but he was glad to be alive. Karen was coming by this morning and he couldn't wait. Yes, she had visited him every day at the hospital, but with all the staff bustling around the wing of the hospital, there was no time for them to be alone.

"Good morning, how's my handsome son?" Curtis smiled as his mother walked into the room with a cup of coffee for him. She brushed his hair back and sat on the corner of his bed.

"Hi, Mom."

She waited for him to sit up before she handed him the cup, "Careful, it's hot. How about some breakfast casserole and some fruit? That sound good?"

Curtis felt like he was 6 years old again. His mom and dad always pampered them when they were sick. Since they were usually healthy kids, that was a rare treat, "Mom, I love you, but I can make my way downstairs."

"Okay, I'll just tell Karen not to worry about bringing that tray upstairs. You're all good, so I'll just tell her to go home."

He saw the laughter in his mom's eyes. "That's not funny, Mom."

"What's not funny?" Karen was standing in the doorway holding a tray.

Abby replied, "Curtis doesn't think his mom is funny."

Karen situated the tray for him, "Abby, I think you can be very funny." She leaned in to kiss the man she loved, "Hi."

She was just beautiful, he thought, "Hi, yourself."

His mom cleared her throat, "I'll just let you two have some time together."

Curtis looked at his mom, whose eyes were sparkling, "Thank you for breakfast Mom." She glanced at him and Karen, who only had eyes for each other. She smiled as she shut the door. As Abby made her way out of Curtis's room, she met her husband on the landing.

"How's our boy this morning, Abby?"

"He's good," She grinned.

"I'm going to check on him."

She steered her husband downstairs, "No, you're not. You're coming downstairs to have breakfast with me."

"Abby, it'll only take a second. I just want to make sure he's okay."

"Owen, right now he's enjoying breakfast while visiting with Karen."

His mouth curved, "Oh well, why didn't you say that in the first place?"

She smiled as they walked down to the kitchen, "I just like messing with you."

Owen stepped up to his wife and touched her hair, "Want to mess with me later tonight, when all the kids have gone to sleep? It'll be like the old days, trying to carve out time for ourselves with a full house." Abby leaned in for a kiss. Owen met her halfway and deepened the kiss. He pulled her in close to him.

"You know, you two do have a room upstairs for this kind of stuff," Leslie walked around them to pour her coffee and threw her dog, Jethro, a treat.

Owen sighed, "See what I mean, Abby? A full house." He hugged his wife and stepped up to the counter to fix their plates and brought them to the table.

Leslie sat down with them. Her mom touched her hand, "It's like old times. It's nice to have you here Honey."

Leslie smiled at her parents, "It's very strange sleeping in this house again. I've gotten so used to being on my own, except for Jethro here for company. It's nice, though. Thanks for breakfast, Mom." Abby nodded and sipped her coffee.

"How's Curtis?" asked Leslie, "I thought he might be sleeping, so I didn't check on him."

"No," mentioned her dad, "he's not asleep. He's having breakfast with Karen upstairs." His daughter gave a half laugh and his dad gave her a look, "Don't you have a business to run?" He looked at his watch. She finished her toast and took a sip of coffee. She walked around to her dad and kissed him on the cheek. Owen eyed his daughter, smiled and gave her a hug, "Just remember, you're cute, but that won't work all the time."

Leslie grabbed her purse and workbag, "Well Dad, I'm 30 and it sure has worked up 'til now." She grinned and waved goodbye.

Owen glanced at his wife, who was smiling, "I blame you, Abby, for her being a smartass." She took their plates to the sink, walked to her husband, and put her mouth on his. His heart raced as he touched her arm. After his wife finished kissing him, he said, "That won't work either."

As she headed upstairs, she turned back to face him, "Well, I'm 57 and it's worked so far."

Owen turned back to the table and sipped his coffee. He grinned and said, "I'm a lucky man."

Meanwhile, upstairs, Karen sat on the edge of the bed, kissing Curtis. She sighed and moved her mouth from his, "I'm so glad you're okay. I've missed you."

He kissed her forehead, "I've missed you too. I want you to promise me you'll be safe."

"I promise. I love you and don't want anything else to happen to either one of us." Karen didn't tell him her plan as she didn't want him to worry. She wanted him to heal, "Listen, Candace is picking me up and I'm going to work for a while."

He put his hand on her arm, "Are you sure that's wise?" Worry showed in his eyes.

She kissed him, "I'm going to be fine. We all will be when this is over." Grogginess began to show on his face, "Okay, I'm going to let you rest."

He caught her hand, pulled her to him, and touched her face, "Take care of yourself, okay? I love you."

She kissed him and picked up his tray, "I love you too." She stopped at the door. He had already drifted off to sleep. She smiled as she looked at the man she loved, "It will all be better soon."

Curtis was pretty much back to his old self, except for the arm. Thank goodness it was his left arm that was sprained. His dad had driven him around the farm so they could check on areas for security and check in with staff. They made sure everyone was secure. He had seen Karen on and off during the week since she was working a lot before the holidays. He couldn't believe Christmas would be here at the end of next week. Curtis had asked his parents to help him with Karen's gift. He hoped she would like it. A smile reached his eyes. Curtis was ready to spend the rest of his life with her.

Karen greeted Detective Myers as he entered the coffee shop, "Miss Smith, you wanted to talk to me?" He nodded at Candace.

"Yes, thank you for meeting me here." Karen talked to the other barista, who was covering for her while she met with the detective, "We can go in back to talk please." The detective followed her to the back kitchen to talk about her plan, "I'd like to try to contact Clarence Higgins and set up a meeting. I'd like you and the police to be there waiting, so when he does try something, you can take him in. I just want this to be over. It's time. He's hurt too many people."

"Miss Smith, we have a search warrant out for him as Miss Marlena Taylor has pressed charges. I don't know if what you are proposing would be a valid idea. Don't you think Clarence Higgins would feel this is a set up?"

"I have to take that chance."

"What does Mr. Dalton have to say about this plan?" Karen was quiet. "He doesn't know about this, does he?" The detective shook his head, "I don't know what it is about you Smith sisters that you feel like you have to handle things on your own without your loved ones knowing about your plans."

Karen took a deep breath, "Probably because we don't want the people we love to be hurt."

"I'll tell you what, Miss Smith. You talk to the team about your plan and when that's done, call me." The detective turned to leave.

Karen took a deep breath and asked, "What if I decide to do it without you?"

Drew Myers stared at Karen and folded his hands, "Let me ask you a question. Why would you want to cause your loved ones grief and pain if something happens to you?"

"It's because of me that Curtis was hurt, and Marlena was beaten. The only way for this to be over is for me to lead the way in contacting him to put an end to his madness and cruelty." She gazed at the detective, "I'm sure Detective Myers, with all the equipment at your disposal, you can get me a contact number for Clarence Higgins."

The detective paced the length of the kitchen with his hands in his pockets. He turned and glanced at Karen, "Tell you what, Miss Smith. You call Curtis Dalton right now and tell him your plan. You also need to call your mother and sister as well. Then, I'll help you with a team of officers on hand." He sat at the kitchen desk, "Your call, Miss Smith."

Karen hugged herself and thought about her plan. She took her phone out of her pocket, "Curtis, hi. I need to talk to you, and I need you to hear me out, please."

Detective Myers made it back to the precinct to make a few calls to finish his shift for the evening. One of the officers came to tell him he had a visitor. Drew waited at his desk. He looked at the young man standing in his doorway, "Mr. Sternum, I was wondering when you were going to see me." He motioned for Wally to have a seat. The detective sat on the edge of his desk, "What can I do for you?"

Wally eyeballed the detective and began to talk.

Chapter 31

Karen was standing in a wooded area at the back of the Dalton farm. It was the Sunday before Christmas. She was more than ready for a good life with her family and friends. Curtis had argued with her when she presented her plan on the phone. He wanted her to have no part in this and felt too many things could go wrong. She listened and told him this was the only way. The darkness of the woods not only held the approach of evil. It contained many good people who were helping her tonight.

"Karen Smith, I almost decided not to show up here tonight," Clarence Higgins III said as he sauntered into the clearing, "I knew it was probably a set up. You're too much of a goody-two-shoes to invite me here for any romantic liaison, but I was intrigued." He pulled out a gun, "Plus, I made sure to look around and sent some friends in ahead of me. By now, all of those people you thought were going to help you in the woods tonight have been taken care of." He walked closer to her. She did everything in her power not to listen to him and not to cringe as he moved towards her.

"Why did you invite me here?" He touched a strand of her hair, "Hmm? Do you know how many times I came close to having you?" He moved closer and smelled her hair, "I was at the beach restaurant that night and happened to see you and your Mr. Dalton there. I hope he was satisfied by you that night." Karen stayed very still. She wasn't going to answer with a response or any expression on her face. Clarence walked around her.

"I also tried to take you from the restaurant that night by the police station, but the cops showed up. Then the coffee shop meeting place didn't happen either. You know if it wasn't for your farm boy, we could have had a nice evening together." He touched her arm with the gun, "So Karen Smith, it's you and me. Whatever should we do?" He laughed maniacally and used his other hand to grab her arm.

"That's enough," Curtis walked out of the woods with a gun pointed at Clarence.

"Well, if it's not the farm boy. Did you want a turn with her too? That's too bad because she's mine tonight. If I were you, I'd put the gun down."

Curtis held the gun in his hand with confidence, "Looks like your friends didn't catch up with us. Right now, they should all be in route to jail."

"It's you against me, Dalton. But I've got the winning lottery ticket right here," He still held Karen by the arm and put the gun to her head.

"Curtis, it's going to be okay." She moved her free hand slightly and covered her heart.

"Listen to her Curtis, it's going to be A-Okay in about 15 minutes when I've had my way with her in front of you." He caressed her hair with the gun, then rested it square in her back.

Karen's eyes held Curtis's. She saw the love in his eyes and said, "It will all be okay."

"Karen, you might want to tell your boyfriend to put the gun down," Clarence said with a smirk on his face.

She replied as she looked at the man she wanted to spend the rest of her life with, "I won't ask him that. I can't ask him to be less than what he is. That's something you will never understand."

"Isn't that sweet? Well, let's get started, shall we?" Clarence held the gun on her back as he began to unbutton the two buttons at the back of her shirt. Curtis held the gun in his hand. It took everything inside him to hold his gun steady. He would follow Karen's plan until he couldn't. He wasn't about to let this deranged man touch her anymore.

She began to wheeze. "Stop that. What's the matter with you?" asked Clarence.

"Inhaler. In my pocket. Have to get it."

"Hurry up," muttered Clarence. "It's time to move on with the show for your boyfriend."

Karen felt the gun move slightly and as she put her hand in her pocket, she pulled out the pepper spray, twisted and shot him in the eyes. Clarence screamed as she ran towards Curtis. She moved in front of Curtis's hand holding the gun.

The man trying to kill them pulled his gun up as Curtis yelled, "Karen!" He shoved her behind him and tried to raise his gun towards Clarence. A bullet slammed into Clarence near his heart and his gun went flying out of his hand as the ground absorbed his fall. Blood was soaking into the dirt from his wound. Curtis helped Karen up and held her tight. He then held her face in his hands and kissed her, "You really took a chance. Why I let you talk me into this, I'll never know."

"You love me. We had faith in each other and our family and friends." They looked around the clearing as those family and friends began to emerge from the woods. Curtis's parents, Ed and Janet, along with Florence, Riley and Hunt were there. Detective Myers came through the woods on the other side with two police officers. Leslie stepped up next to her parents.

Curtis looked at the man who fired the shot that had wounded Clarence Higgins III. Wally Sternum Jr. walked to the man on the ground until he was facing him. He spoke to Clarence, who was still alive gasping for air.

"I just wanted you to know that I'm Wally Sternum, Jr." Wally put his shoe on top of Clarence's wound and pressed down as he screamed. "That's for my sister-in law, Sunny, who you raped after attacking her outside the pizza place she worked at in college. She died after getting hit by the car she was trying to flag down for help." Wally's parents hurried out of the woods. He increased the pressure of his shoe on the wound. Clarence yelled out. Wally continued, "This is for my wife, who was

Sunny's sister. Her name was June, you asshole. She died from grieving for her sister." Wally took his foot off Clarence's chest, "I don't think your daddy's going to help you now." As Wally stepped back still holding his rifle, Clarence started cackling.

"I killed the old man. He was useless!" Blood spilled from his mouth. He turned his head to the side and saw all the people there in the clearing, "You can all go to hell."

One more person emerged from the woods.

Marlena Taylor walked between her parents and into the circle where Clarence could see her, "No, Clarence, that's where you will be." He coughed and then was still.

Wally looked across the way and saw his in-laws, Mr. and Mrs. Gaines, join the group. They looked at the dead man in the dirt. Mr. Gaines nodded to Wally and held Mrs. Gaines as she cried. Wally tried to give the detective his rifle for evidence. He declined as he told him he had lots of witnesses. He had saved Karen and Curtis. Wally looked around the group. He zeroed in on Leslie, who was gazing at him with tears in her eyes. He turned and disappeared through the woods.

Curtis turned to Karen. He pulled her into his arms, "I love you."

She kissed him, "I love you too." She looked at the body of Clarence Higgins III. One thing she knew to be true. Love conquered hate. Curtis put his arm around Karen and led her away to a life together.

Love from Farm to Stable

Epilogue

Curtis was leaning against his truck looking out over the fields. The sun was descending from the sky. His arms surrounded Karen as he held her, "Oh Curtis, it's absolutely beautiful."

He kissed her on top of her head and said, "Wait, there's more." She watched as the sun disappeared below the horizon. The sun left yellow and red colors melding into each other to create a swirl of color.

Karen turned to Curtis and kissed him, "Thank you."

"You're welcome."

"For everything. You've been there for me through this whole horrible time in helping me to heal, supporting me with work and school, and taking care of me when I was sick." She leaned in to kiss him. His lips met hers and he brushed her hair with his hand, "You've been with me every step of the way." Her eyes met his, "I also appreciate your patience in waiting for me." She kissed him.

He touched her cheek and pulled her into his arms. She hugged him tightly and loved him so much. As he held her, Curtis responded, "That's what a good man does when he loves someone and wants to marry her." She leaned back and looked at him. The ring appeared in front of her eyes. His arms moved her back a couple of steps as he knelt down in front of her, "Karen Smith, I love you with all my heart. Will you marry me?"

She nodded her head as tears fell down her face, "Yes. I would love to be your wife."

He stood up. He touched a strand of her hair and put a hand on her cheek. He lowered his mouth to hers and kissed his future bride, "Merry Christmas."

"Merry Christmas. You couldn't have given me a better gift today." She admired the ring sparkling on her finger.

"Well, there is one more thing. Hang on." He went to his truck and came back with a box.

She excitedly opened the box. As she saw the contents, a sigh escaped her, "Seriously, Curtis Dalton?" Karen pulled out an Auburn t-shirt.

He grinned at her, "Just think about what our vows will be; in sickness and in health and football."

"I don't think that's how our vows are supposed to go." She glanced at him, "Hang on a minute. She went to the truck and pulled a box under the blanket she had stashed in the truck, "Here."

He gazed at her with suspicion. He opened the box and pulled out a JAGS t-shirt, "Really, Karen? You expect me to wear this?"

"Well, it goes with these." Karen pulled out JAGS season tickets.

"You expect me to go to the games with you and wear this shirt?"

"Yes, you'll be returning the favor."

He looked at her, "What favor?"

She pulled out an envelope and handed it to him. He opened it only to reveal tickets to the Auburn college playoff game. He spun her around, "Oh my God! Are you serious? Do you know how hard these are to come by?"

"I had a little help from your dad," she moved into his arms, "So, Curtis Dalton, we each give a little in watching our favorite teams. Is it a deal?" She moved back and stuck her hand out.

Curtis looked at the woman he would spend the rest of his life with, "It's a deal." He shook her hand and pulled her back to him. With the stars spread out across the sky against the backdrop of night, the couple in love kissed. After all the struggles and hardships to get to this point, it turned out to be a very Merry Christmas after all.

The End

Look for the 3rd book coming soon in the Over the Bay Series

Love from Farm to Stable

About the Author

Debbie McDonald grew up in Mobile, AL, the youngest of seven children. She has many fond memories of spending time over the bay in the old cinder block house.

Living in Daphne, AL gives her much access to the Eastern Shore and Mobile Bay with the terrific view of the water and beautiful sunsets. She is a wife and mother. She has worked as an Educator for 32 years. Debbie began her writing career in college at the University of South Alabama when her essay was chosen to be included in an English class textbook. She received a check for $25 and a copy of the textbook. It was a highlight of her college career. Over thirty years later, life's experiences led her to write her first book of romantic fiction with more to come in the Over the Bay Series!

Love from Farm to Stable

Resources

Note: If you are a victim of abuse or know someone in an abusive situation, please access the following hotlines for help:

Rape Crisis Center 24-hour crisis line---
251-473-7273

Child Advocacy Center (Mobile, AL) ---
251-432-1101

Penelope House (Domestic violence) 24-hour
crisis line---251-342-8994

Child Advocacy Center (Baldwin County,
Summerdale, AL) ---251-989-2555

National Suicide Prevention Hotline---
1-800-273-8255

Love from Farm to Stable

Tribute to Farmers

Farms.

It's one of the reasons why I live in Baldwin County. I have always loved driving by a farm. The pecan trees, cotton fields, cows, sheep, and horses can all be part of farm life. Who doesn't like to see the corn pop up only to spend the summer eating that corn drenched in butter, trying a recipe for Mexican Street corn or cutting corn off the cob for a dinner of succotash? Devotion, Silver King, and Silver Queen are just some of the varieties waiting to be consumed by customers. Sharing the road with farm equipment is part of everyday life in a farming community. There are songs and movies about farms. There are commercials that take place on farms. Growing up, I have memories of my mother stopping by farm stands and produce markets every summer for tomatoes, lettuce and corn. Sunsets and sunrises are beautiful to see on a farm. At least the characters in this book thought so. I hope you enjoyed the second book in the Over the Bay series.

Please enjoy this tribute to farmers.

Price Pecan Farm Lillian, Alabama

Deborah McDonald

Rockwell Farm Fairhope, Alabama

F&W Farm   Fairhope, Alabama

Deborah McDonald

Manci Farm Daphne, Alabama

Made in the USA
Las Vegas, NV
06 June 2021